Collar Me Crazy

Dragonfly Cove Dog Park

Kay Bratt

Collar Me Crazy

Dragonfly Cove Dog Park Series

Books by Kay Bratt

Hart's Ridge Series:

Hart's Ridge

Lucy in the Sky

In My Life

Borrowed Time

Instant Karma

Nobody Told Me

Hello Goodbye

Starting Over

Blackbird

So This is Christmas

By The Sea trilogy:

True to Me

No Place Too Far

Into the Blue

The Scavenger's Daughters Series:

The Scavenger's Daughters

Tangled Vines

Bitter Winds

Red Skies

The Palest Ink

RED THREAD
PUBLISHING GROUP

This book is a fictional dramatization that includes one incident inspired
by a real event. Facts to support that incident were drawn from a variety of
sources, including published materials and interviews, then altered to fit
into the fictional story. Otherwise, this book contains fictionalized scenes,
composite and representative characters and dialogue, and time
compression, all modified for dramatic and narrative purposes. The views
and opinions expressed in the book are those of the fictional characters
only and do not necessarily reflect or represent the views and opinions held
by individuals on which any of the characters are based.

Chapter One

Dragonfly Cove in April was the best part of the entire year because of the mild weather, and usually Emily Doxon would spend what little free time she could carve out, on the porch, reading a book and dreaming of the day when it would be her name on the spine.

This spring was going to be different, and she doubted she'd be having much reading time. Not unless it involved *how to raise a well-behaved puppy* chapters.

She hesitated before she rang the doorbell. Was she really ready for this? The answer was no, but, since she lived right across the street, it wasn't like she could hide. Leslie wasn't going to let her back out of taking the puppy. She'd already tried twice since it had been born.

She hit the button.

Leslie opened the door with a warm smile, "Hey there, Emily," she greeted, ushering her inside. "I forgot you'd be here first but I'm so glad. My nerves are shot. Want a glass of wine?"

"Sure. White, please." Emily stepped into the cozy living room, glancing around at the familiar surroundings.

Leslie went to the kitchen and returned quickly with two glasses of wine.

As they settled into the comfortable couch, Leslie glanced toward the puppy room. "I've been dreading this moment," she confessed, her voice tinged with sadness. "I'm going to miss this round so much."

Emily followed Leslie's gaze, her heart pounding as she realized she wouldn't be going home alone this time. "You've done an amazing job with them," she complimented, though a hint of uncertainty laced her words. "I just hope I can handle having one of my own. I don't even know how to hold it properly, and I'm worried it'll keep me up all night."

Leslie chuckled; her eyes filled with reassurance. "Don't worry, Em. I've shown you everything you need to know, and the rest is just live and learn. You'll figure it out, and it'll be an incredible journey."

Emily nodded, still feeling a bit apprehensive, but comforted by Leslie's words.

Their conversation shifted toward Leslie's upcoming trip to Italy, and Emily couldn't help but express her concern. "Les, I still can't believe you're going through with this. It's just too risky. What if something goes wrong?"

Leslie sighed, a hint of frustration in her voice. "Emily, please, let's not go over this again. I've made up my mind, and I need this trip. I promise you; Nico is real."

"I just hope you come home in one piece, and not in sections stuffed into a suitcase," Emily said, only half joking.

"On that note, the other families will start arriving soon. Let's get your little girl out of there," Leslie said, then got up. "You wait right here. I'll bring her out."

Emily didn't like to go to the puppy room and get them all stirred up, and Leslie knew that. In just under a minute, she returned with a sleepy, cream-colored pup snuggled up against her neck.

"I'm going to miss this feeling," she said, then gently extracted the dog and placed it in Emily's lap.

The puppy looked up at Emily with a confused look, then turned a few times and settled down and closed her eyes again.

"Thought of a name, yet?" Leslie asked.

Emily stared down at the puppy and stroked her soft ear. She had a lovely splash of white on her chest, something that Leslie said made her "mismarked" and not valued as much as the perfect retriever. She'd given Emily a huge discount to take her.

"Daisy," she said, then looked up at Leslie. "I know it's overused for dogs, but it came to me in a dream, so I feel like it's meant to be. And she's like a yellow flower with a white center, so it works."

"Cute. What else was in the dream? Any sexy Romeo to go with the adorable puppy named Daisy?"

Emily laughed. "No. Jeez, Les. All you think about is romance. What's wrong with you?"

"Um ... I'm lonely? I thought we had that established." She winked. "And soon that will be taken care of. Hey— that reminds me. Before someone else comes, will you help me decide between two of my red dresses? I can't decide to go with the one that has more cleavage, or the one that shows more leg. Come on, I'll show you. Bring your wine."

"Oh, sure, let me help you dress for Naughty Nico," Emily teased. She followed Leslie to the bedroom and Daisy stayed asleep in her arms as she lowered herself onto the bed and put her wine on the nightstand.

She had to admit, it did feel kind of pleasant to have the little thing snuggled up, all warm and soft against her. But she also knew that, once the dog got rested, she'd be wild for a few hours until she settled down again.

That wasn't going to be fun.

Emily had visited plenty of times when Leslie had the puppies out in the backyard, and they were like squirmy creatures on steroids. Always into something.

Leslie went to the closet, talking while she looked through her rack of clothes.

"So, what are you working on while I'm gone?" she asked, her voice muffled.

Emily groaned. "I'm stuck ghostwriting for another health and nutrition coach, and it's so boring. *The Couch Potato's Guide to Veggie Victory* is my current work in progress, and, no—I did not choose that ridiculous title."

Leslie's laughter chortled from the closet. "How do you keep getting these projects?"

Emily smiled. At least one of them was entertained. "Because my name is being passed around in that genre, and now I have three offers waiting."

"Well, just say no," Leslie said, coming out with two dresses over her arm. "You don't have to take the assignments, you know. You are your own boss, Emily."

"I can't just say no. I have bills to pay. It's not like my part-time gig at Barks & Brews is enough to cover me." Emily didn't add that she didn't have a husband currently sending a hefty alimony check, like Leslie did.

Maybe she should've gone ahead and married her ex-fiancé, then dumped him a year later so she could also have a paycheck.

On second thought, even less than another year with

him wouldn't have been worth it. She'd rather be on government assistance if it came to that.

"Which one?" Leslie held the two dresses up, side by side.

"That one," Emily said, pointing to the one without the ruffles around the neck. "It's classier. The other one is too flirty."

"Maybe I *want* to be flirty ..." Leslie batted her eyelashes.

Emily had to admit, Leslie was gorgeous. And very fit for a woman in her mid-to-late fifties. She couldn't believe that her piece of crap husband had left her. If Nico was real, he was going to be very satisfied to see Leslie in person. Maybe too satisfied. She hoped that Leslie came back. She couldn't imagine her life without her. She worked too much to also work on friendships, but Leslie understood that and was fine with a quick chat, glass of wine, or a text here and there when Emily was on a deadline.

"I stand by my choice. Make him earn it."

"You are much too serious." Leslie laughed and took the other dress back to the closet. "Well, what do you want to work on, if it's not health and fitness?" she asked as she came out again, this time with two pairs of heels.

Emily shrugged. "I'd like to write fiction, but I don't even have a platform, and who would want to read my work?"

Leslie leaned in, her eyes filled with encouragement. "Emily, you're an incredible writer, and you have a unique voice. You should consider starting your own project, something you're passionate about. Don't let your talent go to waste putting other people's names on your books."

Emily pondered Leslie's words, a spark of hope igniting within her. "Maybe one day. It's just scary to take that leap of faith, especially when I'm still paying off student loans along with trying to survive. My car is acting up, too. I hope it's just something minor and I don't have to buy a new vehicle. It seems that I can never catch up. I'm going to be writing for someone else forever."

Leslie smiled warmly, topping off Emily's glass. "Don't say that. It'll happen one day, and, when it does, I'll be here to celebrate with you. And speaking of taking leaps, have you been on any dating apps lately? Any good swipes?"

Emily's response was swift and vehement. "Absolutely not, Les! I have no interest in dating right now, especially not online. Anyway, as I told you, I like being single."

That was only halfway true. While it was nice not to have to answer to anyone or go through the ups and downs of navigating a relationship, it was still embarrassing. She was thirty years old and still trying to figure out her career, with no love life on the horizon.

Leslie tilted her head and gave her a knowing look.

She raised her glass in a toast. "Then to new beginnings and pursuing our dreams, in whatever way we want to and whatever they may be."

As they clinked their glasses together, Daisy looked up, then came to her feet on Emily's lap. She squatted and, before Emily could react, a warm circle began spreading on the topside of her blue leggings.

Something told her that it was going to be a long night.

Chapter Two

E ight weeks and a lot of frustrating nights later, Emily was out of breath by the time she'd wrangled Daisy out the door, down the steps, and across the street to Heritage Park. Each time the leash got tangled or fell beneath the puppy, requiring Emily to bend down and pluck Daisy's legs out of it, she sent invisible daggers through the air and over the seas, right to the feet of Leslie, who'd promised she'd be coming right back and had now been gone for eight weeks.

Daisy was officially sixteen weeks old, and it was finally safe to take her out in public without fear of her picking up something to make her sick.

"If you can behave here," Emily told her, "we might even go get a coffee."

Her response was a rapid tail wag. Daisy didn't understand that the coffee would be Emily's reward, if she didn't lose her mind trying to get Daisy to behave for her first time at the park.

Beachside Brews was her favorite coffee shop, and,

since Emily had gotten Daisy, she hadn't been there, or any of her preferred spots around town. Having a puppy wasn't for the faint of heart, that was for sure, especially when your best friend and breeder extraordinaire, who'd promised to help with the hardest weeks in the beginning, was missing in action.

She walked Daisy into the fenced area and unhooked the leash. Daisy immediately took off, her nose to the ground and ears perked at the sudden onslaught of new smells.

Emily went to a picnic table and sat down. Hopefully next time they came, she could bring her laptop and work.

So, maybe Leslie wasn't completely missing in action. She'd called every day in the moments when she could get a moment away from never-ending attention of her darling Nico.

Her mysterious Italian had turned out to be real. Leslie had sent photos of them together, to prove it. The only thing that was not as they'd thought it would be was that Nico was a bit older than his photos had shown.

That fact, combined with the acknowledgement from him that he was infatuated with American women, worried Emily. Was Nico just toying with her best friend? Would Leslie still return to Florida brokenhearted, once the passion and newness wore off?

Another woman stepped through the gates with a mid-size Cavalier King Charles Spaniel and let it loose. It immediately chased after Daisy. Emily was instantly alert.

As much of a pain Daisy was, she didn't want her to get hurt.

"No worries," the woman called out. "He loves puppies."

"Oh, okay. Thank you," Emily returned, still not convinced.

Now the Spaniel had his nose practically up Daisy's butt, nearly lifting her off her back feet. Emily felt like a protective mother and had to squelch the urge to jump off the table and go act like one.

She was saved embarrassing herself by another visitor to the park.

A pretty, dark-haired woman arrived with a yellow retriever that appeared to be about the same age as Daisy. Emily watched them as the woman let the dog off the leash and he scampered off clumsily to join the others in their race around the enclosed area to smell and pee on everything.

The woman looked her way and Emily waved.

It was taken as an invitation.

"Hi," she said, as she approached.

"Morning," Emily replied. "Pretty dog you have there."

"Thanks. Which one is yours?" she looked out at the other two.

"The Retriever, like yours."

Her dog suddenly realized that his owner wasn't behind him, and he raced back.

"It's okay, Charlie," she said. "You can go play. I'm not leaving you."

Emily smiled, then noticed the white marking on his tail. It was shaped like a lightning bolt.

"Is this one of Leslie's Labs?" she asked.

"Yes, it is," the woman said. "Is yours?"

"Yep. Leslie is my best friend, and she harassed me into getting a dog, though I really didn't want one," Emily said, laughing to take the sting out of it.

The woman grimaced. "Sorry?"

"It's okay. She's growing on me. I'll just be glad when she's out of the puppy phase and goes into the calm companion stage of life."

"Aww, I love that they're brother and sister," she said, then rubbed her dog's head. "Go see your sister, Charlie. Go!"

They both laughed. Charlie waited another second or two to see if his owner was coming, then he ran off again, joining up with Daisy and immediately licking her nose. They looked cute together and Emily wondered if they recognized each other.

"I'm not really mad about it," Emily said. "Daisy is sweet, when she's not tearing up things or whining for me to give her attention. I'm Emily, by the way. Emily Doxon." She held her hand out.

"Nora Anderson," she said, and they shook hands politely.

"I don't think I've seen you around," Emily said. "Are you new in town?"

"Yes. Well, I've been here a few months now. Still feel a bit like a fish out of water, though."

"What part of town do you live in?"

"I have a house near the water that I just inherited from my mother. She passed a few months ago."

"I'm so sorry," Emily said.

"Thank you. It's been tough. My life has been quite upside down recently, for a number of reasons. But little Charlie is trying to keep my mind off things. The house wasn't the only thing that my mother left me. She worked directly with Leslie and paid for Charlie, wanting to make sure that, when she was gone, I had someone to fill the gap." She reached up and wiped a tear from her cheek.

"Wow. That's amazing. What a wonderful mom you had. Did you have to leave your job to come here?"

Nora shook her head. "No, not really. I'm a web designer, so I can work from anywhere."

Emily could hear sadness in her voice, but she didn't want to pry.

"I did the same thing," she said instead. "I'm a California girl and decided to try the opposite coast on for size a few years ago. At first it was like living in a foreign country. But now, I love it here. The pace of the east coast is so laid back compared to the west coast."

"Wow, that's a huge move," Nora said. "I didn't come from that far. Just North Carolina. So not that big of a change, except I'm loving being just a walk away from the ocean. It's very soothing. But what do you do?"

"I work at Barks & Brews part-time, and I'm in marketing for my real job," Emily lied. She always faltered to tell anyone she was a writer, because their next question would inevitably be, *what do you write?*

Being a ghostwriter was complicated.

And writing and marketing were kind of the same thing, technically.

"Boring stuff," Emily added.

"Oh, I doubt that," Nora said. "What's Barks & Brews?"

"It's a dog-friendly bar. We even have a park outside for them to run free. You should check it out if you like that kind of scene. We have a lot of live bands, and we host a movie night once a month. Always something going on if you need something to do. Better than staying home alone every weekend."

She didn't mention that staying home alone was something she usually did, anyway. After working her shifts at Barks, she didn't go there often just for fun.

A college-aged girl came into the park, holding a tiny Yorkshire terrier puppy.

Emily and Nora watched as the girl set the pup down and the three other dogs came running, surrounding it while they sniffed.

"That puppy doesn't look old enough to be out in public yet," Emily said.

"I think you're right," Nora replied. "Maybe she doesn't know better."

The girl pulled her phone out and began texting furiously. She looked upset when she finally slid it into her back pocket and came walking up to them.

"Hi," she said, without introducing herself. "Do either of you know of a vet who is open to walk-ins? I think my puppy is sick."

Emily's gut fell. She looked out at Daisy sniffing all up in the puppy's business.

"I use Dr. Sawyer at Bayshore Clinic, but I don't know if they take walk-ins. Maybe give them a call? What seems to be wrong?"

"Do you think she's contagious?" Nora said quickly, nervously eyeing the dog.

The girl looked over at her puppy. "I don't know, but she keeps falling, and she won't eat."

"Falling? Like collapsing?" Emily asked.

"Yes. See, there she goes again!" she pointed at her dog, who had hit the ground with all four legs splayed out as she peered at the dogs above her with a pitiful look.

"Yikes," Emily said. "I don't think you should have her out here this young, especially if she's sick. She might be contagious."

"This young? Why?" the girl asked.

"They aren't supposed to be out in public until all their

vaccines are done and have had time to take effect," Emily said. "My breeder said they are very prone to picking up Parvo, or anything like that, before they are at least sixteen weeks."

"Oh," the girl said. "I just got her a week ago and they didn't tell me that. Hold on, let me go get her. I'm coming, Ladybug!"

She ran over and plucked the dog up, holding it to her chest, then returned.

"Who did you get her from?" Emily asked. Now that the dog was closer, even without a professional eye, it was obvious the dog didn't feel well. She looked like a wilted flower.

"Dogland, over on Pembroke," she said. "She was acting sick just a few days after I got her. But she kept me up last night whining and had diarrhea all over her crate. I called the store about her a few days ago and they said they weren't responsible. I was hoping it would pass and she'd be okay."

"I think you need to get her to the veterinarian, stat," Emily said.

Nora nodded vigorously. "Puppies this little can go down quickly. In a matter of hours, from what I've read. She might need IV fluids."

The girl sighed heavily. "I so don't have time for a sick dog. I've got a heavy school load and a part-time job."

"Then why did you buy her?" Emily asked, feeling perturbed. A dog—and especially a small one like a Yorkie—needed more attention than it sounded like the girl could give her. Even if it was healthy.

The girl rolled her eyes toward the sky. "I hoped I could take her to class with me once I train her to be quiet in a bag. Now I'm stuck with a sick dog, and I can't even afford to take her to a clinic. I'm going to go call the pet store again."

She walked away, pulling her phone out again.

When she was out of hearing distance, Emily turned to Nora.

"That burns my butt. The girl never should've bought that dog. Now if she doesn't get it seen, it might die."

"Maybe the store will take it back, then have it seen by a vet," Nora said.

They waited, and the girl came back, her face red.

"They recommended I take her to emergency care right away," she said.

"What about taking her back?" Emily asked.

The girl shook her head. "Nope. The warranty on their website states it's only for hereditary and congenital issues. Not illness. They said the puppy was well when I got her but, if I had wanted to exchange her for another dog, I've already missed the 48-hour window."

Emily's instinct kicked in. Something wasn't right about that. Especially from a store as popular as the Dogland chain. Now she wondered where they even got their dogs. If it was from a breeder like Leslie, they probably wouldn't even be having this conversation. Leslie's pups were always healthy, and she didn't sell to pet stores, anyway. Leslie cared about her dogs and wanted to know where they were going as well as ensure it was only to responsible owners.

Not a college kid—with no money or time for a pet.

The dog sighed heavily, and her chin dropped to the girl's arm, her head lolling to the side as though she had no control over it.

"I tell you what," Emily said, already irritated with her own bleeding heart. "Take her to Bayshore and see if they'll examine her and give you an estimate of cost for anything else. Then, if you can't afford it, call me and I'll help. I'll give them my card over the phone, but you must get that dog seen right away."

The girl's eyes widened. "Oh my God, you'd do that? You don't even know me."

"I can help, too, if needed," Nora said.

"Give me your phone," Emily said to the girl.

The girl unlocked it and handed it over, and Emily punched her number in. Her phone rang from her pocket.

She handed the phone back to the girl. "There's my number. I'm Emily. Call me when you get there. I'll talk to Dr. Sawyer if you need me to. But please, go now."

"Thank you. I'm Marigold Sanchez, but you can call me Mari. I'll let you know what they said!" She hurried out of the enclosure, then got into her battered Honda Civic and took off.

"Can you believe that?" Emily said, when her taillights disappeared around the corner.

"Young and foolish," Nora said. "I hope they can do something for the poor pup. On that note, tell me how your first weeks with your puppy went. You made it sound like it wasn't too fairytale-like."

Emily laughed. "That's an understatement. Daisy is a pistol. Okay, this is the worst thing she's done ... are you ready?"

Nora's eyes danced and she nodded.

"When I first moved here, I was lonely, but I didn't want to commit to a dog or cat, so I got a hamster. Well, it died. Yeah, I couldn't even keep a hamster alive, which is another reason I didn't want a dog."

"Aww, I'm sure it wasn't your fault. What do you think made it die?"

"Probably lack of attention, though I did try. I just

didn't know what to do with a rodent. Anyway, I buried it in the backyard. Let's just say that my girl might have cadaver-searching instincts because I was deep into work on my laptop, and she showed up and dropped that hamster at my feet. Well, what was left of it. I jumped up and shrieked, dropped my laptop, and a neighbor called it in to the police. A cop showed up and wanted to do a wellness check right in the middle of me giving Daisy a bath to get the stench of death off her, and she jumped from the tub and went streaking through the whole house, rubbing her body on everything she could find. My rug, the couch, my bedding ... all of it. It took me a gallon of carpet shampoo and all sorts of upholstery cleaner to finally get the smell out of my house. And I had to throw away my new rug and all my throw pillows."

Nora's eyes were wide. "I don't know whether to laugh or hug you."

"Ha. I can laugh now, but I wasn't laughing then, I can promise you. I told Leslie that she owes me, big time. She was supposed to stick around and help me with Daisy until I got the hang of things."

"Oh, is she not around? I just talked to her last week."

"Did she call you either super early in the morning or late at night?"

Nora nodded. "Yes, it was early."

"That's because she's calling from Italy. She took a trip and it got extended."

"Oh, well that's nice. But she's still been checking in, so I'm thankful for that. I've never had a dog, so this has been a new experience. Leslie has been good about checking in, even if she's done it from Italy."

"Do you have anyone else at home to help?" Emily asked. "Kids?"

"Not at home. I have a son, but he's nineteen and on his own. My mom's friend Hannah was here with me for the first few weeks to help me settle, but it's just me and Charlie right now. Oh, and my next-door neighbor, I should add. After I caught him sliding Charlie treats through the fence, he introduced himself. He's a huge dog lover, and has been super nice about answering all my random puppy questions."

Again, Emily picked up a wave of sadness with Nora's words. She seemed lonely. Like she needed a friend.

"Have you been to any of the dog-friendly businesses in town yet?" she asked her.

"We stopped by the ice cream shop. Charlie loves their pup cups. Oh, and I met a few others there who have dogs from Charlie's litter. I guess everyone is out and about today since we're at the sixteen-week point."

"I think so, too. I know I've been homebound too much over the last few weeks. Scared to leave Daisy alone for too long. Today I plan to hit the coffee shop and maybe even the bookstore."

"Beach Reads?" Nora asked.

Emily nodded. "Yes. Leo, the store owner, has a dog from this litter, too. I can't wait to see how hers is doing. I'm guessing it will be the smartest of them all, growing up in a bookstore."

Nora laughed. "Probably. Hey—I might see you there. If not, I'm sure we'll run into each other again soon. Either here, or somewhere in town. I've got to run though. I've got a conference call with a client in half an hour. Hopefully Charlie will be so tuckered out that he'll sleep through it and not embarrass me."

"Good luck," Emily said. She watched Nora go collect Charlie and attach his leash before leaving through the gate.

Nora was so nice, and it felt good to make a new friend. However, there was something about Nora that Emily just couldn't put her finger on. She hoped they reconnected because her curiosity about Nora's story was officially stirred.

Chapter Three

The irony that Emily was munching on Oreo cookies while she edited a chapter called "Slaying Snack Attack Monsters" in her current project, *The Couch Potato's Guide to Veggie Victory,* wasn't lost on her. After the succession of health and fitness books she'd ghostwritten in the last few years, she knew quite a bit about eating healthy, but that didn't mean she wanted to do it herself.

Maybe one day, but, for now, the pages filled in a lot faster with an Oreo in her mouth. Or three. The keys clacked on her keyboard as she cranked out the first silly paragraph.

Sitting on the couch, you suddenly feel an all-too-familiar rumble in your stomach. You know that sensation well: the dreaded Snack Attack Monster is rearing its voracious head again. These snack cravings are like relentless beasts, lurking in the corners of your mind, always ready to ambush your willpower. But this time, armed with a plate of crispy carrot sticks and crunchy cucumber slices, and maybe a few of the following more creative options, you will fight back and emerge victorious. The battle against the Snack Attack Monster has officially begun!

As soon as she was done with this chapter, she had to figure out something clever to put in the next one, "Binge-Watching Broccoli." Not that she'd ever take a bowl of broccoli to bed to eat while watching her favorite series, but, again, she was just writing the stuff. Whether the author got bombarded with bad reviews—or broccoli—wasn't her fault.

Miss Fancy Pants Fitness Instructor from Webster, Texas was one of her more Type A clients. She'd given Emily the outline, with the corny chapter titles, and asked her to fill the book in to match. They would send it back and forth to edit the content, and that was going to be less than fun, but Emily aimed to please.

A soft and adorable snore came from the end of her bed.

Daisy was asleep, thank goodness. That meant Emily needed to work as fast as possible before her little demon diva woke up. They'd had a long day with their visit to the park, then the coffee shop, before coming home.

Emily picked up her phone and checked again.

She hadn't heard anything from Marigold, and she couldn't get the sick puppy out of her mind. She wished now that she'd asked its name. It was strange worrying about a dog with no name. *Wait. Ladybug ... didn't I hear her call her dog "Ladybug?"*

That puppy—whatever her name—was pitiful.

She looked at the time on her phone. Four-thirty. The clinic would be closing in half an hour. Surely Mari took her on over there by now.

Everything in Emily told her to count her blessings that she wasn't going to be dragged into anything costly that she couldn't afford. Or any drama. But there was that one little piece of her who had to know what happened. To make sure the dog was okay.

She wrote out a text.

> Mari, this is Emily from the park this
> morning. Did you go to Bayshore?

She hit SEND and immediately saw three dots moving.

> Yes. But too late. She died during
> treatment.

A crying face emoji was next.

Emily dropped the phone. She felt like she'd been gut-punched. But then the phone vibrated. She picked it up before it could wake Daisy. Tiptoeing out of the room, she answered as soon as she'd closed the door behind her.

"Mari, I'm so sorry. What happened? Did they know what she died from? Parvo?" Emily held her breath, hoping it wasn't the dreaded Parvo.

Mari sniffled. "It wasn't Parvo. But she had coccidia, and worms, and fleas so bad that she'd become anemic. He said she had water on the brain and her blood cell count was off the charts. Dr. Sawyer said it was more humane to end her suffering, than to put her through any medical procedures just to probably lose her anyway. Dr. Sawyer didn't charge me anything when he heard my story. He's also going to cover her cremation and give me her ashes."

Daisy whined from the other side of the door and Emily opened it, and dropped to her knees, putting one arm around her dog to cradle her close.

"That's really sad, Mari. Did you call the pet store and tell them?"

"Yes. They don't care. Said I couldn't get any of my money back or a new dog—not that I'd want one from them again, but, still, they should have to do something. Ladybug was sick when I got her home. I just thought it was because she was missing her mother. I should've taken her to the doctor right away, instead of waiting a week. I feel so guilty."

Emily sighed. "Don't feel guilty. You didn't know. You aren't experienced with puppies, and they should've told you what to look out for. No, they shouldn't have sold you a sick dog. It's on them. I think you should file a police report."

"Do you think that's a thing?" Mari asked, sniffling again. "It's not about the money. But I'd love to see them get in trouble. They were so rude to me on the phone."

"I don't know, but we need to find out. How much did you pay for her?"

"Two thousand dollars," Mari whispered. "And that was at a discount because they said she really needed to get into a home for socialization before she got any older. I know it was crazy to pay that much. I took money from my college account and . . . now I have nothing. Poor Ladybug. I should've been better to her."

Emily could hear her start to cry again.

"I tell you what," she said. "Tomorrow first thing I'm going to call up the local precinct and ask them if there's anything you can do. I'll call you after I talk to them. You get some rest and, Mari, listen to me. This was not your fault."

"Okay, I'll try to sleep," Mari said softly. "I keep seeing her little brown eyes. She trusted me to keep her safe."

"Oh, Mari ... I'm so sorry. I'll call you tomorrow." Emily hung the phone up and realized she had her own tears flowing. She put her phone down and picked up Daisy, hugging her closely.

Daisy licked at her tears.

"I'm so sorry for calling you a demon diva," Emily whispered to her. "Thank goodness you are healthy." She rose and carried Daisy to the front door. "How about another walk around the block, just because you're cute?"

She slipped the leash on her, and they went out the door. She still didn't think she was the best one to be raising a puppy, but at least she didn't have to watch her fade away. Mari was going to carry that guilt for a long time.

Anger washed over Emily, and she couldn't wait to find out if there was something they could do to make the pet shop pay for what happened to Mari's puppy. Though money couldn't bring it back, it was the principal of the thing.

Chapter Four

Mari was already inside the Dogland store—and standing in front of a series of small rooms with solid, clear walls with an array of puppies behind them—when Emily arrived and found her. She was carrying a folder of documents.

"Hi," she said, coming up beside her. "Did you already talk to them?"

Mari was staring down at three Yorkshire terrier puppies, all sleeping in a pile amidst the shredded paper on the floor, using each other for warmth and protection. They were even cuter than Daisy as a baby because they were just so tiny. Emily could see why they were so popular. Of course, it had to be comforting to be able to carry them around so easily as they grew older.

She felt a stir of guilt for even thinking it, and silently apologized to Daisy.

"No," Mari said, turning to her. Her eyes were wet with tears. "I didn't want to do it alone. They gave me the run around on the phone so, maybe with you here, I'll get further."

"I'm recording everything they say," Emily said, pulling her phone out.

"I think Florida's a two-party consent state," Mari said, grimacing.

"Oh, crap. You're right." Emily said, putting her phone back in her purse. She looked at the card tacked to the wall next to the enclosure. It listed the breed, the breeder's name and address, city, and state. There was a line for USDA license number, but one wasn't listed for the Yorkies. Below it was another sign offering information on breeders to the customers upon request. She took photos of all the signs.

"Was Ladybug from this same litter?" she asked.

"She was in there with them, so I guess so." Mari shrugged.

"Let's go talk to them."

"Oh my gosh, look at those," Mari said as they passed the next display.

There were six golden pups with a much plumper look than the Yorkies.

Emily peered at the card tacked next to the enclosure.

"Golden Doodles," she said. "I hear about these dogs all the time. People are going crazy for them, and I really don't see why. They're cute as puppies but as adults they look a bit strange to me. Like they're forever in that awkward teenager stage."

There was a license number listed for them. *So why not the Yorkie pups?*

Emily had done a quick internet search of Dogland and found out that they were the only remaining national chain of pet stores that sold puppies in the United States. They were privately owned and based out of Ohio but had franchises throughout several states with over a hundred stores, as well as sixty-some-odd in foreign markets.

She had to admit, it was a nice store. Very professional and clean, and nothing seemed amiss, other than the fact that they'd sold Mari a sick dog. Perhaps it was just a fluke, but, for that kind of investment, they should make it up to her.

The next case showed Chinese pugs, their faces an adorable smooshed-up caricature of a dog. They also had license numbers.

"That's really strange," Emily said.

At the front of the store where the customer service area was located, they waited behind a man returning a bag of open dog food.

"My dog won't eat this food," he complained.

"Of course, sir. Our apologies. Would you like the refund on your credit card or as store credit?"

"Back on my card," he grumbled, handing over his card. "And I guess I have to eat the cost of replacing the rug that my wife won't stop griping about."

"I'm so sorry, sir. You might try taking it to a dry cleaner," she offered.

"They seem very easy to work with, at least in regard to dog food," Emily whispered to Mari.

"Yeah, but two thousand dollars is a big difference than fifty bucks," Mari replied quietly. She looked nervously around her. "Emily, you do the talking, okay?"

Emily nodded and, when the man got his refund, he moved and the girl behind the counter smiled brightly at them. Her nametag said *Dolly*.

She peered at them from beneath long, straight brown hair and round-rimmed glasses.

"Welcome to Dogland. How can I help you?" she asked.

She couldn't have been more than seventeen, and Emily wasn't even going to waste time telling her the whole story.

"We need to speak to the store manager, please."

Dolly lost her smile and pasted on an expression of worry.

"Okay, but, first, can I ask what this is about? Our manager is busy."

"Sure," Emily said, keeping her tone friendly. "It's about a dead dog that your store sold to my friend here. Do you want to explain what happened?"

The girl winced. "Um—let me see if he's available," she said, turning and going into the small room behind her.

They waited quietly and, when Dolly returned, she looked guilty.

"I'm sorry, but he's on a conference call until later this afternoon. He said if you'll leave your name and number, and the paperwork on the dog, he'll call you later today."

Emily could hear Mari's heavy sigh.

"That's not acceptable," Emily said to Dolly, keeping her tone polite and neutral. After all, it wasn't Dolly's fault.

Hopefully.

Mari cleared her voice before speaking. "We need someone to talk to us about this right now. I can't go home and think about this all day. Please."

"I can try to help," Dolly said sweetly.

Mari put the folder down and opened it, pulling out a receipt and sliding it over.

"I called here yesterday about a Yorkshire puppy I bought here last week. I can't remember who I talked to, but I told them she was desperately sick, and they said they couldn't help me, to take her to a clinic. I did that, but Ladybug died during treatment."

Dolly was instantly sympathetic as she stared at the receipt. "Oh, I'm so sorry! I didn't talk to you, but that's what I would've said, too. We don't treat sick dogs here in the store."

"We get that," Emily said. "But the puppy was obviously sick when Mari bought her."

Dolly grimaced and leaned forward. "My manager will just say that you should've brought her back the same day—or within forty-eight hours."

"But I didn't know she was that sick," Mari said. "This is my first puppy. How was I supposed to know?"

"Let me ask you this," Emily said. "Why isn't the USDA license number listed on the card next to the display enclosure of Yorkies over there? Like it is on the others?"

"It isn't?" Dolly asked, looking confused. "Hmm. I'm not sure. I'd have to ask. But I do know that all the breeders we work with are USDA-inspected routinely, and our owner even visits the locations personally. I heard my manager tell someone that, too."

"Oh, so who was the breeder for Mari's dog?" Emily asked. "Do you even know if they came from a reputable breeder? Or was it a puppy mill?"

Dolly looked at the other document in the folder on the counter, then back up at them. "I know our puppies don't come from puppy mills. They aren't kept in little cages and stuff like that, but—hold on—let me text my manager."

She pulled her phone from her pocket and turned away, texting furiously.

When she turned around again, she was smiling.

"He said that those puppies came from Lori Louise Leton, a rescuer based in Valdosta, Georgia. We get lots of puppies from her. She's got a farm-like kind of thing and treats them well. My manager said she's been supplying dogs to us for more than ten years."

"I thought all pet store dogs come from breeders?" Emily said.

Dolly shook her head. "I know they mostly come from breeders, but she's a rescue. I—I'm really not sure how it works, to be honest."

"Why do they come all the way from Georgia?" Mari said. "Aren't there dogs available in Florida? Rescues and breeders?"

"I'm not sure about that, either" Dolly said. "But we also have dogs that come from breeders in Missouri and Ohio. I guess that we work with the best ones, no matter how far away they are."

"Has your manager personally seen the rescue facility?" Emily asked. Ohio made sense, considering that was where the Dogland headquarters was located. But why Georgia? "Or have you?"

"I haven't, no. Hold on." Dolly texted again, and when a reply came through, she nodded. "He said yes—he's seen it, and they are legitimate. They have routine exercise schedules and even retirement plans for the puppy moms and dads. He said she wouldn't supply us with a sick dog, and it must've been something the puppy got into at your house."

"She didn't get into anything at my house," Mari said. "I know that for a fact. I never had my eyes off her unless she was safely in her crate."

"That's really screwed up of your manager to say that to her," Emily said. "As if she isn't sad enough, now he's trying to blame her."

"He said he's sorry," Dolly offered again, tilting her head in an annoying way.

"*I'm sorry?*" Emily repeated, feeling anger wash through her. "That's all he has for her? My friend paid thousands of dollars to spend one week with a sick dog.

Someone is going to have to do better than *I'm sorry*, and we aren't leaving until they do. So, you can tell your cowardly manager if he has time to text, he has time to come out here and face us. We aren't leaving until he does."

"Right," Mari agreed. "We aren't leaving. Ladybug deserves an answer, too."

Dolly looked really worried now. She twisted a long lock of hair around her fingers.

"Um ... okay. I'll go tell him, but he's not going to like it. What is your name?"

"Marigold Sanchez. And this is my friend, Emily."

When Dolly whirled around and went back into the office, Emily shook her head.

"I can't believe the gall of that manager," she said. "He won't even come out and speak to you. Something is not right here. I can feel it."

"I agree," Mari said.

A line of customers had built up behind them, waiting for service, and Emily could hear two of them grumbling to each other.

Dolly returned; her face serious.

She leaned over the counter toward them.

"I'm sorry," she whispered, "but he says now you are causing a disruption to the store and that, if you don't leave, he'll call the police and have you removed from the store. Coming back here would be considered trespassing. But he still plans on contacting you later about your dog."

Emily turned to Mari. "What do you want to do?"

Mari looked alarmed. "I don't know. I really need that money back, but I also don't want to be arrested. That wouldn't look good on future applications."

Emily wasn't ready to give up. They were not causing a disruption. They'd been nothing but cordial and profes-

sional. How could they be removed—and considered tres-
passers—for asking for a refund, or at least an explanation
about the dog?

The manager was bluffing.

But Mari was sweating bullets.

"Okay. Leave the folder with me and you go on. I'm not
leaving," Emily said to her. "I'll call you later."

She turned back to Dolly, smiling in an overly polite
fashion.

"Go ahead and wait on these nice people behind me. I'll
just sit right over here." She picked up the folder, then went
to the end of the counter and hopped up, crossed her legs,
and jiggled her feet.

Her mama always did say that she had a stubborn streak
a mile wide. Emily just hoped this time it didn't result in
handcuffs.

Chapter Five

Half an hour later, Sean Broadnax, the manager of Dogland, finally emerged from his office, looking tense and harried. His appearance matched Emily's expectations perfectly—a middle-aged man in rumpled slacks and a white button up, his receding hairline adding to his stern countenance. His eyes darted around the store, assessing the situation, his lips pressed into a thin line.

Meanwhile, Emily maintained her defiant stance at the counter, her stubbornness unwavering. She had no intention of leaving until they received satisfactory answers about Mari's dog, and hopefully at least a partial refund.

Broadnax didn't attempt to speak to Emily. He stood there, arms crossed and staring anywhere but at her. Dolly made herself busy, wiping the counter around her register.

As the tension mounted, the sound of approaching footsteps and the jingling of keys signaled the arrival of a uniformed police officer. Emily glanced over her shoulder to see him entering the store. He was tall and ruggedly handsome. Dark, tousled hair and piercing blue eyes that seemed to miss nothing. His neatly trimmed beard framed a strong jaw and confident expression, which contrasted sharply with the frazzled atmosphere of the store.

Emily had recently binged on the *Yellowstone* series during a writer's block, and the cop was giving off strong Rip Wheeler vibes. Women all over the nation were fawning over Rip more than his co-star, John Dutton, played by the famous Kevin Costner, because of Rip's no-nonsense masculinity and rough edges.

She hopped off the counter and put a polite smile on her face.

The officer approached Sean Broadnax, extending a firm handshake. "Mr. Broadnax, I'm Officer Kuno Fischer from the Dragonfly Cove Police Department," he introduced himself. "I understand there's a situation here that requires our attention?"

Sean Broadnax nodded, his expression still stern but somewhat relieved to see the arrival of law enforcement. "Yes, Officer Fischer. This woman and her friend, who already took off, have been causing a disruption in my store. This one," he gestured Emily's way, "refuses to leave, even after I explained that I would contact the customer later regarding her concerns."

Officer Fischer turned his attention to Emily, his gaze sweeping over her calm and determined face before facing Broadnax again, his eyebrows arched in surprise.

"She doesn't seem to be disrupting anything. Can you be more specific? What exactly did she do?"

Broadnax blustered, his face turning red. "She's stopped now since you're here. Let's not get into specifics. I just want her to leave and get her ticketed for trespassing, so she and her friend don't return. She caused a scene, and I don't need that here around the other customers. Dolly here can tell you." He took a step back, putting Dolly into the hot seat.

"I—well, her dog died. I mean, her friend's dog died," she said, looking from her manager to the officer. "She was upset, but they didn't raise their voice or anything like that. They just wanted to talk to the manager."

Emily maintained her silence, waiting her turn.

The officer nodded calmly. "Gotcha. I've heard your side, now let me talk to her."

He turned to Emily and nodded for her to go ahead.

She tried to maintain her dignity in her words. "Officer, my friend and I were not disruptive. We asked to talk to the manager, and he hid in the office like a yellow-bellied snake."

"Well," the officer looked like he was trying to suppress a grin at her description. He gestured toward Broadnax, "He's here now. So, talk."

Broadnax interrupted before she could do so.

"This young lady's friend purchased a Yorkshire puppy from our store last week. Unfortunately, the puppy fell ill, and she took it to a clinic, where it passed away during treatment. She called here to the store, seeking a refund, but I explained that we don't provide refunds for sick puppies outside of our forty-eight-hour window. Obviously, she wasn't happy with that answer because here we are. However, I assured her that I would contact her later today to discuss the matter further."

"You didn't assure her of anything," Emily said. "You wouldn't come out of your office."

He ignored her, keeping his eyes on the officer. "The message was given by Dolly here. I know that I'm going to be harassed about a refund again, but she will not be getting her money back. She should've brought the dog back immediately."

Suddenly Mari reappeared next to Emily and apologized under her breath before she turned her attention to the officer.

"Officer, I'm the one who bought the puppy. I didn't know she was that sick until day four or five, and it's not just about the money; it's about ensuring that other people don't go through what we did," she said.

"Exactly," Emily agreed, so proud of Mari for coming back. "Also, on the placard next to the other puppies that we think are from the same litter, there is not a breeder's USDA license number listed, as I understand is store policy. It's kind of fishy considering that one of the dogs died a week after leaving this store and now we can't even check out where it came from, don't you think? Our concerns are legitimate. And I agree, it isn't about the money but let's not forget that you charged two thousand dollars to a struggling college student for a dog that lived only a week."

The officer appeared sympathetic. He considered their words, his eyes briefly flicking to Sean Broadnax. "Mr. Broadnax, can you provide a brief explanation of why there isn't a USDA license number listed as Mrs. ...?"

"Miss. It's Miss Doxon," Emily said.

"As *Miss* Doxon says," he finished.

Broadnax sighed. "Certainly, Officer Fischer. Those pups didn't come from a breeder. They came from an official rescue with a nonprofit 501(c)(3)."

"Can you give them the information?" Fischer asked.

"Here it is," Dolly said, sliding a piece of paper over. "I already wrote it down for her."

Broadnax shot her a look that said he wasn't happy with her.

The officer took the paper. He sensed Dolly's discomfort and directed his next question to Mari. "Ma'am, I appreciate your passion for this matter, but, if the store manager has promised to address your concerns, it might be best to allow him to do so through the proper channels."

Mari met his gaze with a mix of determination and frustration.

Officer Fischer continued, holding his hand up. "Wait a second. Hear me out. I understand that this is a complicated situation. However, I'd like to suggest a compromise. You ladies will leave the store now, without further disruption, and you, Mr. Broadnax, will contact them no later than six o'clock tomorrow evening to address their concerns in a timely manner."

Sean Broadnax hesitated but eventually nodded in agreement. "Very well, Officer Fischer. I will call them tomorrow."

Emily, although reluctant to back down completely, understood that it was the best course of action for now. She exchanged a glance with Mari, who nodded in resignation. "Okay," Emily said, placing the folder on the counter. "We'll leave for now, but we expect a call tomorrow."

Officer Fischer smiled reassuringly. "Thank you for your cooperation, ladies. I'm confident that Mr. Broadnax will follow through on his commitment."

He shot Broadnax a warning glance.

With that, Emily and Mari exited the store, leaving behind a lingering tension and unresolved questions.

As they stepped out into the bright sunlight, Emily couldn't help but feel a sense of unease.

"He's a jerk," Emily said.

"I hope you aren't talking about me."

They turned to find Officer Fischer right on their heels, a big smile on his face.

"I'm sorry. No, we were talking about the manager, Officer Fischer."

"Please—call me Kuno," he said.

"Emily, I'm going to take off," Mari said. "I'll call you later."

Mari left her standing there with the officer. He still wore the smile, looking at her quite strangely.

"You said *Miss Doxon*, right?" he asked softly.

His statement threw her off for a second.

"Oh. Yeah. Single. Not married," she said, waving her left hand at him, then feeling like an idiot. She might be single, but she wasn't yet ready to mingle, and now he probably thought she was implying she was interested.

He nodded slowly, obviously amused. "I was just asking for my report."

Emily could feel the heat rush up her neck and into her cheeks, and she wished the concrete would open and swallow her.

"Oh," was all she could think to say.

"And here's that information on the rescue," he said. "I didn't have a chance to give it to your friend."

"Thank you," Emily said, taking it and tucking it into her purse. She noticed he wasn't wearing a wedding band. Not that she was looking. "I'll give it to Mari."

"So, you live around here?"

Emily moved her weight from one foot to the other, feeling awkward. "Yeah. Not too far. But actually, I have my own puppy at home, and I'd better get back before she tears something else up."

She took a few more steps toward her car.

"Okay," he said, looking stern again, and walking with her. "Did you get your dog here at this store, too?"

She shook her head vehemently. "No way. Mine is from a reputable breeder here in town."

"Well, I'm sorry about your friend's dog. I was going to tell her that, but she seemed in a hurry. Please let me know if you don't hear from the manager with a satisfactory result. I may not be able to get her two thousand back, depending on the store rules, but I can put some pressure on him to give her another dog. I'd try, at least."

"Thank you," Emily said. "That's really nice of you to care."

Another dog for Mari would probably help her heartache, but they couldn't let this go; they needed to get to the bottom of what had happened to Ladybug and ensure accountability for future pet owners who dealt with Dogland.

Kuno handed her a business card with *Dragonfly Cove Police Department* printed across the top.

"Call me. Anytime," he said.

She could smell his cologne, an outdoorsy scent of cedarwood and clove. It was intoxicating, and she realized that she hadn't even showered yet that morning. Daisy had kept her busy with her antics until it was too late, and she'd had to run out the door looking like a homeless person in sweats and an oversized T-shirt.

"Will do," she said with too much energy in her tone.

Why was she so awkward with the opposite sex? She didn't used to be that way, but her ex had ruined her, taking away every ounce of self-confidence she'd ever had. She quickly got into her car, keeping her eyes anywhere but on Officer Kuno as he stood watching her, his arms crossed over his chest and a big smile across his face.

Chapter Six

Emily returned home only to find that Daisy was still in her crate, but she'd chewed a hole through the Lamb Chop stuffie and was now sitting in a nest of cotton puffs, looking proud of herself.

"Daisy," Emily scolded. "That was your favorite toy. Now what are you going to do?"

She opened the crate and led Daisy to the back door, opening it and pointing to the grass.

"Go potty," she said firmly.

Daisy's tail wagged furiously as she stared up at Emily. She wanted attention, but Leslie had said not to give her any positive reinforcement until she eliminated after being let out of her crate.

Daisy whined and Emily turned her back to her.

Finally, out of the corner of her eye, she saw Daisy sigh, then go squat in the grass.

"Good girl!" Emily exclaimed, clapping her hands, and squatting so that she could hug her wiggling body. "Now, let's go clean up your crate. You know, you're going to have to learn to settle in there when I'm away, and stop being destructive."

She hoped that eventually Daisy could roam free in the house when alone. She hated putting her in the crate. If they'd ever make that goal, it would probably take a miracle.

Daisy was so antsy and nervous.

When she'd finished picking up the Lamb Chop guts and stuffing it back into its body, she got a needle and thread and did a quick hack job of sewing it back up. She tossed it back to Daisy, who was delighted in the resurrection of her favorite Lamb Chop.

"Now go play while I call your real mom," Emily said, taking her phone to the couch and settling into the corner, her legs tucked under her. It was just after five in the evening in Italy, so hopefully a good time to catch Leslie before dinner.

She dialed Leslie's number, but it went straight to voicemail. She left a message telling her to call when she had time. She wanted to talk to her about Mari and the pet store and get her take on what they could do.

Suddenly she remembered that she had the name of the rescue that provided Ladybug to Dogland. She drew it from her pocket.

Leton Legacy Paws & Claws Rescue.

She pulled her laptop over and keyed it into her search bar along with the words *dog rescue*. Nothing came up on the first page, so she went to the next.

Not a single hit.

On the floor, Daisy fell dramatically at her feet, rolling

over and putting her feet in the air. She whined and then gave a little yap.

"Not now, Daisy."

Emily remembered that Dolly said the name was Lori Louise Leton, so she searched for that while Daisy settled in, her nose digging into Emily's foot as she chewed at a toy she'd placed on it.

"Could you take that somewhere else, Daisy?" she asked, absentmindedly with her gaze glued to her computer screen.

She opened Facebook and tried there.

A page with that name came up in the search. Emily scrolled down to the *About* section. It read:

Leton Legacy Paws & Claws Rescue is a nonprofit 501 (c)(3) organization made up of a small group of people who devote and dedicate their love, time, and personal resources 7 days a week, 365 days per year, to care for homeless, abused, and abandoned animals.

Considering that Dolly said they'd been getting dogs from that rescue for at least a decade, the page only had about a dozen posts, so appeared to be new. The photos showed dogs that appeared to be healthy, and none of them showed much of a background for Emily to get an idea of what the premises looked like.

Something wasn't sitting right with Emily.

On the left sidebar, in the Intro box, it listed the page as a nonprofit organization in Valdosta, Georgia, but no street address. There was a phone number listed under that and Emily picked up her phone and dialed it.

It went directly to voicemail with a message stating that they weren't available by phone but please leave a message, and that they could also be reached with any questions or requests by emailing them at the listed email address.

Emily put the phone down, sighing heavily.

She went back to the Facebook page and read the post pinned to the top.

We have a favor to ask. We're in need of a few items for the dogs in our rescue. Mostly grooming supplies and small collars. We also need a couple types of food and a few other items. Any help is appreciated and will really help our dogs. Thanks in advance for any support you can offer!

It gave the link to a wish list on Amazon's shopping site.

Emily clicked on it to find pages of items listed; everything from dog food to dog toys and even small, plastic pools and puppy pads. Much more than just a *few items*.

She went back to Facebook, and the next post was from someone named Veronica Jones from six months before. In the photo she was holding a small, white dog, with a caption that thanked Lori Louise for her new baby. The dog was definitely a puppy and didn't look like a rescue. It appeared healthy and cheerful.

She clicked on Veronica's name and went to her profile page.

At first, she didn't see any photos of the dog, but, as she kept scrolling, she got to one that showed the pup and said, "Please pray for Chewy, he's not feeling well. Vet in the morning." But no update.

Emily hesitated but decided to go for it. She was already emotionally invested so she clicked the message button and wrote a short note.

Hi, Veronica. You don't know me, but I saw your post on the Leton Legacy rescue page from several months ago. I see that you got Chewy from the Leton rescue, and just wondered if you recommend their services and if you could give me the address where the rescue is located?

She hit SEND and sat back, staring at the photo.

When a reply didn't immediately come back, she did another internet search for the rescue, flipping through more pages of results, but none of them showed Leton Legacy Paws & Claws specifically.

There were a lot of similar names using the words *Paws & Claws*, but not with Leton.

Her messenger dinged and Emily opened it, excited to see a reply from Veronica.

> No, I do not recommend them and do not want to be involved. You can find their place out on Ousley Road. Don't mention my name.

Before Emily could write back, the screen glitched and she saw that Veronica had blocked her.

"Well, that's interesting, don't you think, Daisy?" She looked down and instantly felt her face blush with irritation.

Daisy stared up at her with innocent eyes, then opened her mouth as if grinning. Emily looked closer and saw that the toy that she'd *thought* was keeping Daisy engrossed atop her sneaker *was* her sneaker!

Daisy had chewed off her shoelaces and made a nickel-sized hole in the canvas.

"No, no, no ... Nikes are not chew toys," Emily whined. But she couldn't say too much. If she hadn't had her head stuck in her screen for so long, she would've noticed and could've redirected Daisy to a real toy.

And this was why she didn't want a dog. She checked her phone again to see if Leslie had texted her back yet. It was time they talked about a better situation for Daisy. With someone who had more time. And patience.

But nothing awaited her in her messages.

She wondered if Mari had heard from Sean Broadnax yet, but decided to take Daisy outside while she made that call. She slapped the lid of her laptop down and set it aside. She also needed to get to work on the next chapter of her current project. She had a title.

"Binge-Watching with Broccoli." Now she needed some filler but that was hard to come up with from a person who had a long-standing war with broccoli as far back as Gerber foods and highchairs. But she'd think of something.

And she needed to change her shoes. She wondered if the warranty covered dog tears.

"You are so naughty," she grumbled down at the culprit.

Daisy was still smiling, and she tilted her head. Her eyes danced and she seemed to be saying, *maybe so, but the joke is on you.*

Chapter Seven

E mily opened the back door and lifted Daisy up onto the seat. She clicked the dog safety belt to her harness and shut the door. She and Mari settled into the front seat and the engine roared to life.

"Let's do this," Emily said, pulling out of the parking lot where Mari's apartment was located.

The Dogland manager had not tried to get in touch with Mari, and Emily had lay awake all night, not being able to get Ladybug out of her mind. Her thoughts had jumped around, making her feel dizzy with confusion and possibilities until she'd rose at six in the morning and called Mari.

"How about a road trip?" she asked.

"It's Wednesday. I have class, but I might be tempted. Where do you want to go?" Mari had replied.

"Georgia. Play hooky and let's go check out this so-called rescue that your dog came from. Something tells me there's more to the story."

Emily picked her up at eight sharp. That was the earliest that Mari would budge, and she still wasn't ready when Emily and Daisy showed up at her door.

Mari ushered them inside, telling them to get comfortable while she slapped on some makeup. Finally, on the way down to the car, she'd also negotiated Starbucks, telling Emily that they could get Daisy a pup cup.

"Absolutely not," Emily said. "My luck, it would go through her like water and be all over my backseat. But I'll spring for your drink."

At the first window, the girl hadn't even flinched when Mari ordered, but it made Emily's head spin. "I want a Grande Hot Flat White with a triple shot of espresso and nonfat milk, extra foam but only on the bottom half of the cup. Add one pump of vanilla syrup, one and a half pumps of caramel syrup, and a sprinkle of cinnamon on top. Then, in a separate cup, add two pumps of hazelnut syrup to a splash of nonfat milk, with a drizzle of caramel on the inside of the cup. Serve the flat white and separate milk mixture on the side and add a packet of Equal sweetener on the side as well." Then she looked at Emily, gesturing it was her turn.

"Just an iced Caramel Macchiato for me, please," Emily said, then gave Mari an incredulous look.

"What?" Mari asked, laughing.

"You know what. That's a very complicated drink for a girl living on a tight budget. Is that your regular?"

"Gosh, no. I only get Starbucks if I pass an exam with a B or higher, as a reward. But since you said you're paying ... well ..." she let her voice trail off, then giggled again.

She looked so happy about her order that Emily didn't mind so much.

They got the coffees at the next window, then got on the road.

The GPS said that Valdosta, Georgia, was going to be a three-hour drive.

Daisy had finally settled down and looked like she was going to take a nap. Emily was relieved; maybe her dog would end up being a good car rider.

According to her online preliminary search, they'd follow Highway 75 into Georgia where it would turn into SR 31. After a while, they'd turn on Rocky Ford Road, and it would run into Ousley. From there she didn't know whether to take east or west, but it didn't appear to be a very long road, so they were going to look until they found the place.

Or at least that was the plan.

Emily had always considered herself directionally challenged and didn't know what she would've done if she'd have begun driving before phones and GPS. Her parents and even her ex had teased her relentlessly that she could manage to get lost in a paper sack.

Then again, they didn't have much confidence in any of her skills. She couldn't blame them. Here she was thirty years old and still trying to be a novelist. And paying her bills by writing boring stuff for others and supplementing her budget with waiting tables.

That sure didn't make her look like a rocket scientist. She should be doing better by this age, not still scrambling.

She did better now with directions than she used to, and, after all, she did find her way from one coast to another to settle into her new life in Florida a few years back. She wondered what her ex thought about that, and felt just a touch of pride that she'd been brave enough to do it, and lucky enough to figure it out. Either that or she'd had an angel on her shoulder, guiding the way away from him, out of the darkness and into the light.

She also couldn't read a map all that well, but her route today appeared to be very simple.

Mari was the first to break the silence. She leaned back in her seat, letting out a sigh as the miles stretched ahead of them. "So, Emily, I guess you're wondering a bit more about me, huh?"

Emily glanced over at her new friend. "What do you mean?"

"I mean, you already think I'm a young, immature idiot who paid too much for a dog, especially a sick one." She sounded glum.

"Now, I didn't say that," Emily said, though it felt like Mari had read her mind. "I mean, I know you're in college, and you mentioned you have a part-time job, but I'd love to hear more about you. We'll have about six hours on the road today, so no better time to do it."

Mari gave a wry smile. "Well, I'm your typical, broke college student, working hard to make ends meet. I'm studying social work, actually. It's kind of ironic considering my own history."

Emily raised an eyebrow, intrigued. "History? What do you mean?"

Mari took a deep breath before starting her story. "I grew up in the foster care system, bounced from one home to another. My biological parents had their own issues and couldn't take care of me. It was tough, you know? Never really having a place to call home."

Emily felt a pang of empathy for Mari. She herself had grown up in a loving household, surrounded by her parents and siblings. The contrast between their upbringings couldn't have been starker. "I can't even imagine how challenging that must have been for you."

Mari nodded, her eyes distant, looking out her window as she continued. "When I turned eighteen, I aged out of the foster system. The state provides a small stipend, but it's barely enough to cover tuition. I still have rent, utilities, and necessities because I chose to cut ties with the state. That's why I have a part-time job in addition to going to classes. I'm determined to make something of my life, and social work feels like the right path for me."

"What about siblings? Or other relatives? Do you have any family at all?" Emily asked.

"Nope. None that I'll claim. They're a bunch of leeches and I cut ties with them a long time ago. I'd rather be an orphan than claim them as my family."

Emily was moved by Mari's resilience and determination. "You're incredibly strong, Mari. I admire your commitment to building a better future for yourself."

Mari smiled gratefully. "Thanks. I won't lie—it's been a rough journey. When you look like me—dark eyes and hair, brown skin—it's a lot different than being blonde and blue-eyed like you. Everything is harder. But I'm not one to give up easily. I sort of walk this world alone. I never made friends easily, and I don't have time to try now. That's why Ladybug meant so much to me. She was going to be more than just a dog; she was supposed to be my companion, my friend, in a world where I feel so alone."

Emily's heart ached for Mari. She now understood why Mari had been willing to spend so much on a dog, even if it had ended tragically. Ladybug had been more than a pet; she had been a source of comfort and companionship for someone who had faced unimaginable challenges. She was right, too. There was no doubt that anyone with brown skin had to work a lot harder to get to where they wanted to be in this world. It wasn't fair.

"I get it now," Emily said softly. "I understand why Ladybug was so important to you. And why you want to make sure this doesn't happen to anyone else."

Mari nodded, her eyes glistening with unshed tears. "Exactly. I know I look tough, but I've been devastated. I can't stop thinking about her. She was so sweet and innocent. I don't want anyone else to go through this."

"I agree. And if we can uncover the truth about where those puppies really came from, it might prevent others from being hurt. Dogs *and* people," Emily said. As the silence grew around them again, she reflected on the privilege she had taken for granted—her loving family, her stable upbringing, and her financial security. Sure, she'd had heartbreak, but it was only a short chapter in her life.

"Thanks for helping me," Mari said. "I don't know why you are so interested, but I'm glad."

Mari's whole life seemed full of disappointments. Her story fueled Emily's determination to help her find justice for Ladybug.

"Because I'm the type to do the right thing," Emily said, her voice soft. "Not only that, but—if you think you could squeeze me in—I'd love to be your friend. I mean—nothing too weird or mushy," she joked.

Mari laughed. "Yeah, I can handle that. If you get too soft, I'll just give you some of the tough love I grew up on. That'll put you on the right path. Now, let's talk about you. I want to hear all your adventures in high school and college. Tell me you weren't always this straitlaced, please."

Chapter Eight

Two hours into their drive, Emily couldn't help but feel a growing sense of camaraderie with Mari. The miles had rolled by quickly, and the conversation flowed easily between them. Emily had managed to make Mari laugh with some of her teenage escapades, which she had once thought were rebellious but were nothing compared to the ones Mari bounced back at her, things she and other girls had done in foster care.

"You were so vanilla," Mari exclaimed.

"What the heck is that?"

"Um ... the opposite of what I was. Let's just leave it at that. Thank goodness I straightened up when I realized that blowing up my own life wasn't hurting anyone but me."

"Good point. But I've saved the best for last. Want to hear my wildest tale?" Emily chuckled, glancing at her friend.

Mari grinned, her eyes brightening. "Absolutely! Lay it on me."

Emily cleared her throat, recollecting her teenage years.

"Well, there was this one time when my friends and I decided to sneak out of my house to go to a midnight screening of a movie. We broke curfew."

Mari laughed, shaking her head. "That's it? Breaking curfew? That's your wildest teenage story?"

Emily blushed a bit, realizing how tame her teenage antics had been in comparison. "Okay, okay, maybe that wasn't so wild. But that reminds me, after our movie escapade, we formed a secret club, the 'Midnight Society.' We'd sneak out and gather in my backyard to tell spooky stories with a flashlight under the full moon."

Mari burst into laughter, her amusement infectious. "Oh, you were a true rebel, weren't you? Jeez, at thirteen I could throw back a bottle of Jack and smoke a pack of cigarettes by midnight, and that's after sneaking out my second-floor window to sit on the roof."

Emily joined in the laughter, feeling a warmth between them. "Well, I thought so at the time, but I've got nothing on you. Tell me more of the crazy stuff you had to deal with in foster care."

Mari's expression sobered, and she leaned back in her seat. "Oh, there were definitely some wild moments, but not in a fun way. Imagine constantly moving from one place to another, never knowing if the next family would be kind or cruel. Eventually I learned to adapt, to blend in, and to stop drawing attention to myself. Those skills kept me safe, once I figured it out."

Emily listened intently. "That must have been incredibly tough. I can't even imagine what that must have been like."

Mari nodded, her eyes distant as she recalled her past. "Yeah, it was. But it's made me strong and resilient. And it's why I want to make a difference in the lives of others who've faced similar challenges. If I ever graduate, I mean. It's not helping that I'm not in class today. This better be worth it."

"I can't promise that, but at least you and I are closer. Now I'll have to treat you like a little sister and you'll probably bug the crap out of me. But since I started it, I won't be able to say a word," Emily said, winking at Mari.

Mari smiled appreciatively, and the conversation shifted to lighter topics as they continued their journey.

In the backseat, Daisy whined and jumped to her feet, peering out the window, then whining again.

"She must have to potty," Emily said. She drove another mile until she saw a church with a big, empty parking lot, and pulled in.

Daisy was full of herself by the time Emily parked and opened the back door to put the leash on her, and she jumped right out, before the hook clicked. She took off running.

"Daisy, no!" Emily screamed. They were close to the highway, and she could just see the tragedy unfolding in her imagination.

Mari jumped out, too, and they both began chasing Daisy. Each time Daisy would stop somewhere to sniff, they'd get closer, and she'd run off again. So far, she hadn't headed toward the road, but Emily was exhausted and in tears, worried half to death.

"Just stop," Mari said, holding her hands up to Emily. "If we sit down, maybe she'll come to us."

Emily doubted that. Mari didn't realize how wild Daisy was, but, at this point, she needed to sit down. Her legs were like jelly and her heart was pounding out of her chest. She followed Mari to the church steps, keeping one eye on

Daisy who watched her with a mischievous expression as she trotted from tree to tree near the children's play area.

When they both sat down, Daisy stopped.

She tilted her head at them, looking confused.

"I know what to do," Mari said. "Play dead."

"Play dead?" Emily repeated back to her. "Are you crazy?"

"No, I saw this on TikTok. Do what I do." She stood, let out an agonized cry, then crumpled to the ground.

Emily laughed. But she wasn't sold on falling to the cement. She was older than Mari and sure wouldn't recover as easily.

Mari opened one eye. "Come on, do it," she hissed at her.

"This is ridiculous," Emily sighed, but did her best to follow Mari's acting job. She fell a lot more gently than her younger counterpart, but she outdid herself with a pitiful cry for help.

They lay there, Emily holding tightly to the leash, staring up at the sky, with Mari suppressing giggles. "What's she doing now?" she asked. Her head was pointed the opposite way, and she couldn't see Daisy.

Emily peeked.

"She's still standing there looking at us like we've lost our minds. She's confused."

"Stay dead," Mari said.

It only took another minute or so before Daisy got concerned enough to prance over and put her sloppy muzzle in Emily's face, checking for breath.

Emily quickly grabbed her around the neck, sat up, and hooked the leash.

"You are such a bad girl," she said.

"No, don't tell her she's bad. She came to you to see if you were okay," Mari insisted.

"Fine. But she is. Come on, Daisy. You've had enough exercise to last the whole day and half of tomorrow." She got her back into the car and, though she was beyond irritated, she offered her some water from the small thermos she'd brought.

Daisy licked it up furiously, then settled down, looking like she was ready for another nap. They got back on the road.

As they approached Valdosta, Emily couldn't help but feel grateful for the bond she and Mari were forming. She'd made two new friends in as many days. Nora and Mari. Maybe now she wouldn't feel so lonely with Leslie gone.

An hour later, the GPS led them to a four-way stop where a street sign read *Ousley Road*.

"This is it," Emily said. "But do we go left or right?"

"Let's try right."

Emily turned and they continued driving on Ousley Road, which seemed to twist and turn endlessly. The dense trees on either side of the road created an eerie canopy, casting shadows that played tricks on their eyes.

"Maybe we should turn around and try the other way," Mari said, after a good twenty minutes.

"It's not a long road either way, so let's keep on until it turns into something else, then we'll turn around."

Now silent with concentration, they kept driving until Emily saw another, smaller dirt road coming out just beyond a grove of trees.

"Hey, look at that," she said, pointing toward the side road. "That doesn't show up on the GPS, but it might be worth checking out."

Mari nodded in agreement. "Let's see where it leads."

Emily turned onto the dirt road, the car's tires crunching on the uneven surface. The path was rough, and they bounced along as they ventured deeper into the unknown. They passed a big sign stating *No Trespassing* but kept going.

Soon, they came upon a clearing that revealed an old, massive metal building, surrounded by several smaller outbuildings that resembled dilapidated chicken coops, boosted into the air on wooden stilts.

The place seemed abandoned, but the air was filled with an overwhelming stench of neglect and suffering.

"What is this place?" Emily whispered nervously. Behind her, Daisy whined.

Mari looked equally anxious as they parked the car at a safe distance. She wrinkled her nose. "I have no idea, but it smells awful. Surely this isn't it."

"Let's make sure, since we already drove way down here," Emily said. She cut off the car and, after telling Daisy to stay put, they got out and cautiously approached the grim structure. There were no signs of life around, no people to be seen.

As they reached the windows of the main building, they peered inside and were met with a shocking sight.

They'd found Leton Legacy Paws & Claws Rescue. But it didn't look like what Emily felt a rescue place should look. It was dismal and the conditions were deplorable. Dogs of various breeds were crammed into filthy, overcrowded cages, their feet precariously perched on wire bottoms. The animals within view appeared malnourished, their fur matted and dirty.

Closer to the window, the air was thicker with the stench of urine and feces.

"Oh my God," Emily whispered, her heart breaking as

she took in the sight of the suffering dogs. "This is ... this is inhumane."

They backed away from the window and walked over to one of the structures that favored a chicken coop on stilts.

The first one was empty, but, when Emily peered into the second one, she was speechless with horror. It held a full-grown German Shepherd. A quick glance told her it was male, and the dog was standing on the wire floor, trembling. His coat was patchy with bald spots and his eyes were rimmed with red, and so hollow and sad. Even though he was so thin you could count his ribs, he still looked too big to be able to go through the small door that led to the interior den area.

He watched them, his head lowered in fear.

One of his paws was bloody, an injury obviously from his balancing on the wire, the rusty metal going through his foot pad and splitting it painfully.

Mari's eyes welled up with tears, her voice shaking with anger and sadness. "We need to call the police, Emily. This can't be legal."

Emily swallowed the lump in her throat. She hesitated for a moment, torn between the urgency of the situation and a thought that crossed her mind. She wanted to free the dog. Let it out of the horrible cage, take it somewhere—or something.

But a German Shepherd was valuable. Maybe even the value of a felony if caught taking him. It would be just her luck for them to get caught in the middle of the act.

"Wait, let's call Officer Kuno. He might know what to do."

As she was about to reach for her phone, they heard the unmistakable sound of a car approaching on the gravel road, out of sight. Panic surged through them, and, without a word, they retreated to their car and Emily hastily continued down the driveway, then around the building, taking the opposite direction to avoid being seen.

The car on the gravel road grew closer, and her heart pounded in her chest as she steered the car onto the main highway. Everything in her wanted to stay there and confront whoever had arrived, but she'd brought Mari along, and it was her duty to keep her safe. She wouldn't jeopardize the girl.

"What're we going to do?" Mari asked.

"I don't know. Let's go get some lunch and talk about it."

Still reeling from the encounter at the rundown dog rescue, Emily and Mari pulled into an eatery called Bubba Jax Crab Shack. Mari chose it, and the Yelp reviews were mixed, but they were drawn by the promise of good food at reasonable prices. As well as somewhere to think about their next steps. On the way over, Mari had used Emily's phone to fire off a text to Officer Kuno, asking him to call when he got a chance.

Now they had time to kill as they waited.

Mari took Daisy and found a table outside, while Emily headed in to tell them they were there, and to use the restroom.

The rustic charm of the place welcomed her as she stepped inside. The place had a distinctly local feel, with beer served in bottles, drinks in Styrofoam cups, and food on paper plates with cheap plastic forks. The decor seemed to be frozen in time, a throwback to the 1960s, and the restrooms had clearly seen better days. But none of that deterred Emily, as they were there for one thing—the food.

After alerting the host that they'd taken a table outside, Emily went to the restroom, then returned to Mari and Daisy.

The server came and they placed their orders, Emily opting for a pound of perfectly boiled peel and eat shrimp with homemade cocktail sauce, while Mari went for a shrimp plate that came with hush puppies and two sides.

As they got comfortable at the worn table with metal chairs, Emily's phone vibrated in her pocket. She quickly glanced at the screen and saw that she had a missed call from Officer Kuno Fischer. She excused herself from the table, taking her phone with her to return the call.

"Hello, Officer Fischer," Emily said when Kuno answered the phone. "I mean, Officer Kuno."

"Just Kuno. Nice to hear from you, Emily, but what's going on? Your message seemed urgent." Kuno's voice held a note of concern. "More trouble with Broadnax?"

"No. We haven't talked to him yet. We're in Georgia," Emily replied, feeling a mixture of guilt and frustration.

"Who is we're? And why Georgia? What are you doing there?"

Emily took a deep breath, knowing she needed to explain. "Mari and me. And my dog, Daisy. Remember, it's her puppy that died? We came to check out the place where Ladybug supposedly came from. It's a dog rescue, I guess you could say, but the conditions are terrible. I want to report them."

"Wait a minute. Were you invited to come on to the property?" He asked, concern in his voice.

"I—well, not really. No. We were not. To be honest, there was a no trespassing sign, but we ignored it."

Kuno sighed audibly. "Emily, you can't just trespass on private property like that. It's not only illegal, but it's dangerous. Ever hear of the Stand Your Ground law in Georgia? It gets twisted all the time and people get shot just for stepping foot somewhere uninvited."

"I know, I know," Emily said, her frustration bubbling up. "But listen. I don't think what they—at that place—are doing is legal. I mean, there must be laws against those kinds of conditions for animals, and why is a big chain pet store like Dogland getting their puppies from a place like that? Something isn't right. You must admit that."

"Without seeing it myself, I can't admit anything," he said. "I tell you what, you two come back. I'll make some calls to my friends in Georgia, and they'll investigate this properly. But it'll take some time to go through the right channels. No one is going in there with guns and badges blazing. This isn't a Netflix movie, Emily."

"I know that, Officer Kuno. But let me tell you about the shepherd." She filled him in on the dog's physical appearance and his living conditions.

He sighed heavily on his end of the phone. "That sounds appalling, but, again, this must be done the right way. You can't go back there."

Emily's anger flared, and she snapped, "So you want me to just leave town and let those animals keep suffering while the wheels of justice turn ever so slowly? And never know if something was done?" She thought of the German Shepherd, his eyes filled with confusion and pain. "No," she continued. "If you can't promise me this will be looked at urgently, I'll go back there by myself right now. I can't stand by and do nothing."

Kuno's voice softened. "Listen, Emily. I understand your concern, but there are people whose jobs it is to handle these situations. For now, I need you to come back to Florida. It's not safe for you to go there again, especially if they are trying to hide something. You could get hurt or even be arrested if you go back."

Emily leaned against the building, moving her feet out of the way for a happy couple to get by and go inside.

"That's fine. I'll go to jail for the benefit of helping those dogs. I could only see a handful, but the ones we saw were miserable."

Kuno paused for a moment, and then he spoke calmly, "Emily, I promise I'll look into this today. But only if you don't go back there. I don't want you putting yourself or Mari at risk. If she gets a record, she's going to have a tough time when she gets out of school. Don't you think?"

She saw Mari peering her way, trying to see where she'd gone. The girl had been through a lot to get to the place she'd made for herself. She was doing good, a law-abiding citizen, getting an education to make a difference in the world.

Reluctantly, Emily agreed, her concern for Mari's safety outweighing her anger. "Okay, fine. I'll come back home. But you better make sure those dogs get the help they need, and I want you to call me immediately after you've gotten in touch with someone. Keep me in the loop."

Kuno's tone softened again. "I will. Thank you for listening to me. Be safe on your way back, okay?"

As Emily ended the call and headed back to the table, she tried to calm herself. She was going to have to sell it to Mari that Kuno was going to do something about the situation. And she had to break it to her that their escapade was over, and, after they fed their faces, they had to get back to real life.

Chapter Nine

On Friday night, Emily was halfway through a four-hour shift at Barks & Brews when her phone vibrated in her pocket. She set the tray of appetizers she was carrying down on an empty table and pulled the phone out and looked at the text.

> Break time yet? I'm at a table near the first gate.

It was Officer Kuno.

Emily shook her head, already feeling irritated. He'd kept in touch, but, other than some paper pushing, so far nothing had really been done about what she and Mari had discovered in Georgia. As far as she knew, it wasn't shut down, and that was the only result she'd be satisfied with.

But maybe he had good news. She texted him back, telling him to give her a few minutes, then she quickly delivered the appetizers to the waiting table, then put their order into the computer. She asked Katie, another server, to finish them out, then she grabbed a tall glass of water and hustled over to find Kuno looking relaxed in a pair of jeans and a long-sleeved T-shirt, nursing a craft beer, and picking at a tray of chicken wings.

He smiled when he saw her and waved her to sit down.

"Hi," he said. "Want some wings?"

"What's up? Anything new to report?" Emily got to the point, even as she looked out over the closest dog yard and spotted Daisy, lying on her back next to a Basset Hound. She was loving her first visit to accompany Emily to work.

Kuno laughed. "Slow your roll. Can't we exchange pleasantries first?"

"I'd rather hear that something is happening to shut down that horror house of a rescue, and, no, I don't eat chicken wings. Have you seen those trucks that carry those poor chickens to slaughter? Feathers blowing out everywhere and the hens trying to slip through the wire to escape?"

He shook his head calmly. "No, can't say that I have. But about the case. Emily, I told you. These things take time."

She sighed loudly and took a drink of her water.

"We've done everything you said to do. It's not fair that it's this slow," she said, when she'd wet her mouth.

He nodded. "I know you have. And you're doing things the legal way, which will keep you and Mari out of trouble. That's the most important thing."

"No, it's not. The most important thing is doing something for those animals."

Through Kuno's coaching, Mari had filed a *puppy buyer complaint form* with the National Humane Society online, a step that tracks problem pet sellers and hopefully would initiate further action. Emily had called the Valdosta Humane Society, told them what they'd found, and requested they go inspect the facility. The girl who answered the phone said she'd pass the information on to her supervisor.

"I talked to my buddy at the Lowndes County Sheriff's Department, and he said they are slammed right now, but he'll try to get out there sometime next week," Kuno said.

"I don't even know if that German Shepherd will make it to next week. I told you, he looked bad."

Kuno shook his head sadly. "I'm so sorry. I know it's really weighing on you."

"Yes, it is. And that jerk Broadnax from Dogland never did really give an answer as to why he sold Mari a sick dog. He finally offered her five hundred dollars to drop the complaint and let it go."

"Did she take it?"

"Nope. I'm proud of her. She's taking the complaint on up the ladder to the corporate office. Oh, and I talked to Leslie, my breeder friend. She said that Dogland is one of the only two national pet store chains in the United States that still sell puppies. The rest of them have been stopped from doing it."

"I wonder how they still get away with it," Kuno said.

"I don't know because I was doing some digging and found a report from a few years ago in which dead animals were found in freezers at five of their stores. They'd let them die rather than get them to veterinary care."

Kuno grimaced and put down the chicken wing he was chewing. "That's horrifying. What kind of animals?"

"Dogs and bunnies. Kittens. I also found a class action lawsuit against them that's pending."

"For?" Kuno asked.

"It alleges that Dogland stores charge premium prices for puppies and kittens they "certify" to be healthy — as claimed by their own veterinarians — when in fact they are selling animals prone to illnesses and other defects, due to their sourcing from mills that churn them out as fast as they can. It also contends that the stores further inflate their prices with phony services and warranties that cannot be claimed."

"And it's still pending?" He picked up his wing again and nibbled.

She nodded. "It said the court granted the defendants' motions to dismiss the case a year ago, but the Animal Legal Defense Fund has appealed it to the 11th Circuit Court of Appeals."

"Good," Kuno said, then picked up his napkin and wiped his mouth. He held a finger up to Katie, indicating to bring him another beer.

"Yeah, maybe, but they can drag class action suits out for years. Who knows if they'll ever shut it down. It's depressing." She tapped at the table with her nails, then immediately hid them in her lap. She needed a manicure desperately.

"Can we talk about other things?" Kuno asked, smiling. "You said you were struggling to finish a writing project. How's that going?"

He looked devilishly debonair, and he probably knew it.

Emily groaned, remembering that she'd told him about it in one of the several phone calls he'd made to her over the last few days.

"It's going. Slow and painfully," she said. "I'm working on a chapter called 'Potato Power: A Guide to Spud Supremacy.'"

He laughed. "Do you even like potatoes?"

"Oh, yes. I love potatoes. Any way they come; baked, fried, mashed. Potatoes are one of my favorite foods."

"Same. But I prefer them made into French fries."

Even as they talked about food, Emily couldn't stop thinking about the dogs in Georgia. If only Kuno could've seen them with his own eyes, he might be just as alarmed as she and Mari were. She wished she had the power to shut it down herself. Or at least free some of the dogs.

"What are you daydreaming about?" he asked.

She snapped back to reality. "I think you can guess."

He looked sympathetic. "Well, how about letting me take you out to dinner when your shift is over. Anywhere you want. My treat. That should get your mind off things."

Now she was really back in reality. He'd just asked her out!

"I—I—um ..." she stumbled over her words. She couldn't remember the last time someone had asked her on a date.

"Jeez, don't look so pleased about it," Kuno said, letting out a nervous laugh. "Am I that hideous?"

Ha. That was a joke. He was beyond good looking and had the bad boy thing going on, too, even though he was a cop. He was also too much of the total package to be interested in her.

"No, not at all," she finally croaked out. "It's just been a long time since I've dated. I really appreciate the offer, but I'm tired after my shifts end. And I need to get Daisy home. She's been here the whole time and will be ready for bed. Rain check?"

He looked sad, but he gave her a thumbs up.

"All this talk about dogs, and I forgot to ask you if you have one?" Emily asked, staring out at the dogs playing in the enclosed area.

"Nah," he said. "I'm not really a dog person."

"Cats?" she asked, raising her eyebrows. "Somehow I don't peg you as a cat man, either."

He chuckled. "You're right. I don't do cats. If I were to

have a pet, it'd be a dog, but I'm just not ready for that kind of commitment."

Hmm ... he was commitment-phobic, it sounded like.

So was her ex, and Emily had given him way too much of her youth, only to have it backfire when it was time to get serious.

"Do you have to work tomorrow?" he asked after a few seconds of silence.

"Not here," Emily answered. "But I really need to finish the rough draft of this book so the author can go back in and do her thing, then send it to me for editing. I don't get paid until it's done."

He smiled. "Don't tell me, tomorrow you're tackling a chapter on bean sprouts."

"Ha. Nope. Don't laugh, but it's called 'Zucchini Zen: Finding Inner Peace Through Veggies.'" She said it with a straight face, though it was a struggle.

He put his hand over his mouth and apologized through it, then burst out laughing. She had to agree with him—her chapter titles were beyond ridiculous. But it was what her client wanted, and she aimed to please. Her car insurance was coming up.

"Hey, that's not nice," she said, pretending to be mad. "I put a lot of work into coming up with that one."

He apologized again, but his laughter was entertaining to watch. His eyes were watering, and he wiped at them as he tried to get himself under control.

She felt the nerves leave her body and she giggled with him, glad he wasn't upset that she'd turned down his offer of a date.

A friend who liked to laugh she could handle.

A romantic date, not so much.

Chapter Ten

Saturday morning Emily was still in her pajamas and slippers, moving through the house like a slug. She'd slept fitfully and was still tired from her shift the night before, but headed toward the coffee maker to give herself a boost when her doorbell rang.

Quick as a ninja, she hid behind the kitchen wall, hoping whoever it was hadn't seen her through the glass on her front door.

Who would be coming over so early? Emily wasn't expecting anyone and never had impromptu visitors, except for Leslie, and, as of her text messages from the day before, she was still in Italy enjoying her new man.

She stayed close to the hallway wall and crept up to her door and peered through the peephole. She was surprised to see Officer Kuno Fischer standing there. How did he even know where she lived?

Panic washed over her. She hadn't had time to tidy up or even change out of her pajamas.

Emily quickly tried to flatten her unruly hair and

straighten her sleep-rumpled clothing, but there was only so much she could do in a matter of seconds.

With a sigh of resignation, she opened the door to find Kuno standing there in a uniform that wasn't his usual police attire.

"Good morning, Emily," Kuno greeted her with a friendly smile and two cups of steaming coffee. He held one out to her. "I guessed and had them add cream and sugar."

"Uh, hi," Emily replied, feeling a flush of embarrassment. She leaned against the door frame, pretending she wasn't in her night clothes and looking like a character in a sitcom. "Thank you, I guess. What brings you here so early?"

"Can I come in?" Kuno cleared his throat and glanced around before leaning in closer. "I did some detective work after our conversation yesterday, and I found something interesting."

She stood aside. "Yes, but, first, how did you know where I live?"

He waggled his eyebrows at her. "I'm a police officer. It's our job to investigate."

She smiled. She had to admit, her curiosity was piqued. She beckoned for him to come in and led him to the kitchen, then to the table. "What did you find?"

Kuno took a seat. "The address for that dog rescue in Georgia is the same as an address for a breeder who was shut down after multiple offenses more than two years ago."

Her eyes widened. "Are you serious?"

Kuno nodded solemnly. "Dead serious. The breeder went by a different name, but it's possibly connected."

"So, what's the plan?" she asked, feeling a surge of hope.

Kuno hesitated for a moment before replying, "I'm going to go visit them undercover today, posing as a

USDA inspector. I want to see if it's the same people running it."

Her excitement was tempered by worry, but she felt the thrill of the chase taking hold of her. "I want to go with you. I can be 'in training' with a clipboard, khaki pants, and a button-up shirt. I won't interfere; I promise."

Kuno hesitated, but ultimately relented, a hint of a smile on his face. "Alright, you can come, but you have to promise to stay out of trouble. If we get there and I feel like it's too dangerous for you to get out of the car, you'll stay put. Okay? I'm jeopardizing my position over this. We have to be careful."

Emily agreed readily, her heart pounding with anticipation.

She quickly made a call to Mari, leaving a message for her to come by and let Daisy out to potty later in the day, explaining that she and Kuno were heading back to Valdosta on a mission and that she'd fill her in later.

Kuno took Daisy out to the backyard and exercised her while Emily got dressed. She then put her in the crate, tucked the door key under the front mat, and they were off.

As they drove, Kuno explained, "I found the address listed as a breeder on the annual Horrible Hundred report from the National Humane Society. The kennel had been cited by USDA inspectors for repeated Animal Welfare Act regulation violations for sick and injured animals and other problems."

"What is the Horrible Hundred report?" she asked, afraid to know.

Kuno glanced at her and explained, "The Horrible Hundred report is a list of known, problematic puppy breeding and/or puppy brokering facilities. It's not a list of all puppy mills, nor is it a list of the worst puppy mills in the country. Instead, it's a list of dog breeders that should be avoided."

She got her phone out and quickly searched the report, finding it in the first page of hits. She opened the file and began reading, and instantly felt sick at her stomach.

He continued as she read, "They provide the updated report annually, not as an all-inclusive inventory, but as an effort to inform the public about common, recurring problems at puppy mills. The information demonstrates the scope of the puppy mill problem in America today, with specific examples of the types of violations that researchers have found at such facilities. It serves as a warning to consumers about the inhumane conditions that so many puppy buyers inadvertently support."

She was reading those specific examples, and it was disgusting. What people would do for money was sickening.

When she got to the last of the list, she shut off her phone. The Horrible Hundred report was a sobering reminder of the widespread issues in the dog breeding industry, and she was more determined now than ever to make a difference for the suffering animals they had encountered. But her mind raced with the implications of what they might discover.

Kuno continued, "At this location's most recent inspection September before last, the kennel was cited for two bulldogs in need of veterinary care, including one who had 'green drainage' coming from the eye and another whose eye was 'red with drainage.' They also found puppies stacked in wire cages, deep in excessive feces."

Emily winced at the horrific details, her heart aching for the suffering animals. She was grateful that Kuno was willing to investigate further, even if it meant putting himself and his job at risk.

"Let's talk about something else," Kuno said. "You're looking kind of green over there."

He was right. It was a lot to take in.

"Okay. What made you decide to become a cop?" she asked.

"Oh, that's easy." Kuno began to talk about his childhood and his desire to become a police officer like his grandfather was, and he spoke of how proud his dad was when Kuno earned his badge.

Emily listened attentively, finding herself drawn to his stories and the glimpses of his past. She asked about some memorable arrests he'd made, and he entertained her with some he found amusing, until they were both laughing at his descriptions.

The miles sped by faster than lightning and, when they arrived at the location, Emily's heart raced with anticipation.

"It doesn't look like anyone is here," Kuno said.

"That's how it was when we were here."

"I'm sure they have a caretaker stop by daily to tend to the animals," he said. "Let's go take a look."

They got out of the car.

"First you have to see the German Shepherd," Emily said. She led him to the chicken coop-like enclosure on stilts.

The dog was still there. Still balancing awkwardly on the wire floor in an obvious attempt to keep his foot pads in the least painful position possible.

"Oh, man ..." Kuno said.

The situation was even more heart-wrenching than before. The dog looked worse than ever, emaciated and weak, with pleading eyes that seemed to beg for help.

"Whoever put him in this is a piece of ..." he trailed off,

mumbling under his breath as he unlatched the door of the coop.

Emily felt tears welling up in her own eyes as he gently guided the dog out of the enclosure and set him on the ground.

The German Shepherd's legs seemed unsteady, as if he had never walked on solid ground before. He wobbled for a moment, then collapsed. When he laid on his side, the sight of his red and raw testicles made Emily flinch.

"There's no water in there either," Kuno said angrily.

Emily rushed to the car to fetch her water thermos, desperate to provide some comfort to the suffering animal.

"What are we going to do with him?" Emily asked as she returned and offered the dog some water.

He lapped at it slowly, as though he didn't have the strength to drink.

Kuno looked at the dog with determination. "We're not putting him back in there, that's for sure. If he runs away, so be it. He deserves his freedom after living in that prison and probably siring litter after litter to fill someone's greedy pockets."

"It doesn't look like he plans to go anywhere," Emily said. "Nor does he have the strength."

They gave him a few more reassuring pats and then turned their attention to the large metal building.

The door was locked, but it only took Kuno less than a minute to jimmy the lock.

"If someone comes, I'll say we heard a dog yelping in distress," he said.

As they entered the facility, the stench and the appalling conditions hit them like a wave. From wall to wall, dogs were held in overcrowded, filthy cages. The building itself had poor ventilation, and Emily suppressed her urge to gag.

The sight was overwhelming, and Emily and Kuno went around and took photos with their phones to document the horrors.

In one corner, Emily looked down into a pen to find an emaciated mama Boxer with her puppies at her feet. The pups were crying erratically, pleading for their mom to lower herself back down where they could reach. The only thing keeping the dogs from the concrete floor was a soiled and thin pink blanket. The mama looked up at her with sad eyes. Emily could see her raw teats, baggy and hanging low to the ground.

She looked too thin to be able to produce enough milk for six pups, and that was probably why her pups were hysterical.

"I'm so sorry, girl," Emily muttered, and reached in to rub the dog's ears, then she noticed that the pen was full of feces, and maggots crawled around the top of one pile.

This time she couldn't help it. She gagged and ran outside.

When she got her breath back, she returned inside.

Kuno was still snapping photos, and using his phone to dictate a report of what he was seeing. He was at another pen, but this one was cleaner and held six French Bulldogs.

"Oh, they're watching out for these, since they are the big money-makers right now," Emily said. "Each one can go for five grand or more around Atlanta and other big cities."

As they moved deeper into the facility, Emily's eyes burned, and she felt a growing sense of unease. She'd stopped taking photos so that she could hold the top of her shirt over her mouth. The conditions were beyond deplorable, and the dogs' suffering was evident.

"I think I have enough," Kuno said, turning to her.

"Then let's get out of here." There were too many dogs to help right now, and she was ready to take the next step in shutting the hell hole down.

But suddenly, a door opened so hard it slammed back against the wall and a man rushed in, holding a shotgun. He was dressed from head to toe in camouflage, muddy work boots completing the outfit of a certified Georgia country boy.

"Stay where you are," he shouted, aiming the shotgun right at them.

Chapter Eleven

Emily's heart raced as Kuno pushed her behind him, creating a protective barrier between her and the armed man who had suddenly appeared.

"Let me do the talking," Kuno whispered to her.

In a calm but authoritative tone, he introduced himself, "I'm Jeffery Baner, USDA inspector, called out to do a surprise inspection due to a call from an anonymous whistleblower. The door was unlocked, and I heard a dog in dire distress, so I entered the facility. Who *are* you and why are you pointing a gun at me?"

The man's grip on the shotgun seemed to loosen slightly as he replied, "I'm Ronald Gettlefinger. We had a break-in last month and twenty dogs were stolen. I thought they'd come back."

Kuno wasted no time and instructed firmly, "Put the gun away."

Reluctantly, Ronald complied, dropping it to his side, and the tension in the room eased slightly. Emily let her breath out, feeling relief.

"Are you licensed to carry?" Kuno asked him.

"Sure am."

Kuno came forward and pressed further, asking, "Do you know Lori Louise Leton of Leton Legacy Paws and Claws?"

Ronald nodded; his nervousness palpable. "Yeah, she's my mother. She's the founder of this enterprise."

"Well, that's an interesting way to describe it. I thought it was a rescue?" Kuno's voice remained steady.

"Yeah—it is. Enterprise, rescue. Same thing." The hand he held the gun with was shaking next to his knee. "Correction. I'm the founder of the rescue."

Kuno shot Emily a confused look before continuing.

"Well, can I ask how it's possible that this same address is listed with a breeder that used the name Leton Kennels, and was shut down for multiple offenses of animal cruelty?"

"I—um ..." Ronald stammered.

Kuno didn't let him finish. "From what I'm seeing here, it appears that when your mother's breeder license was revoked, and this place closed, she filed for a $501(c)(3)$ approval to open her own rescue. Or under your name, as it seems. And with some kind of miracle, or possibly money changing hands where it shouldn't, it was approved. And you two barely missed a lick before you were back in the puppy mill business."

Ronald shifted uncomfortably, glancing around. Kuno's controlled anger was evident, but he maintained his composure. Kuno continued, confronting Ronald about the deplorable condition of the dogs, and listing things they'd found in the horrendous environment that was posing as a rescue.

Ronald argued, "It's not a puppy mill. We take care of our animals."

Emily nearly choked on her outrage.

He noticed and said, "What? They all have food, water, and shelter."

"Not all of them. What about the German Shepherd outside?" Kuno pointed out, raising his voice slightly. "Is he being cared for sufficiently? How many more breeder dogs do you have hidden around the property, holed up in horrific enclosures just waiting until you're ready to breed them again?"

Emily wanted to speak up, but Kuno had instructed her to let him do the talking.

Ronald mumbled something about retiring the shepherd, but Kuno countered, "Oh. So now that he's too old to make you money, he doesn't deserve his dignity?"

Ronald's defensive demeanor began to crumble as Kuno pressed him with more questions and accusations. Ronald whined, pleading with them not to file incident reports, explaining that his mother would be furious if she found out.

Kuno, still maintaining his firm stance, asked, "Where is this mother of yours?"

Ronald nervously shuffled his feet, glancing back at the building and then back at Kuno. "She's out of town. She entrusted the business to me until she returns."

Emily whispered to Kuno, "Maybe we should just get out of here, document everything we've seen, and get someone down here to shut this hell hole down."

Kuno nodded, acknowledging her suggestion, but continued to engage with Ronald. "We will have to file the reports and provide the photos to officials," he stated firmly.

Ronald, clearly distressed, followed them outside, pacing nervously. "Is there anything we can work out to keep you from doing that? If we lose our 501(c)(3) status, we'll have no livelihood. I've got four kids to feed."

Emily couldn't help herself, and her frustration slipped out as she retorted, "Maybe you should have thought about that before you started delving into animal cruelty."

"I guess that tells you what you want to know," Kuno said, winking at Ronald. "No, there's nothing you can do to keep us from filing a detailed report. We don't want your bribery. Keep your money for bail because you can expect to see law enforcement out here as soon as we can get to them and make our case."

Ronald used his sleeve to wipe the perspiration from his forehead.

Emily followed Kuno to his truck, and they climbed in. She felt like she needed to burn the clothes she was wearing, as well as take a bleach bath. They were just about to pull away from the nightmarish scene when Emily's gaze went to the shepherd.

Her heart ached for him, so battered and weak. He looked like he'd given up on life.

Kuno put the truck in reverse.

Suddenly, the German Shepherd looked toward them and began to fight to get to his feet. The first try was an epic failure, and he fell.

He tried again, his watery eyes never leaving the truck as he struggled.

Emily realized that from somewhere deep within his broken body, the dog was pulling out his last ounce of strength, trying to save himself.

Alarmed, she exclaimed to Kuno, "He's trying to get to us."

"Ronald?" Kuno asked, turning around.

"No! The German Shepherd!"

Kuno looked and, in the next second, he slammed the

truck back into park and climbed out. Ronald was still standing there, watching them.

The dog had made it up and was on his feet when Kuno reached him. Despite the warm, spring day, the dog was trembling violently, but he was standing.

Kuno bent down and looked into his eyes. Emily couldn't hear what he said. Then the dog took one wobbly step toward Kuno, before falling again.

"What are you doing over there?" Ronald called out from behind him. "You can't take my dog."

"The hell I can't," Kuno yelled. "This dog is going to die if someone doesn't do something for him right now, and I'm sure not depending on you to do the right thing."

With utmost care, he lifted the frail dog, cradling him in his arms. As he carried him around to Emily's side of the truck, she opened the door, her eyes overflowing with tears.

As she watched Kuno being so gentle with the dog, something within her moved. She had to admit, a man with that much compassion toward an animal he wasn't even familiar with was probably capable of being a pretty good date, too.

She wondered if he'd ask her again.

Kuno carefully placed the dog in her lap and then retrieved a blanket from behind his seat, carefully tucking it around the shivering canine. Leaning down next to his ear, he whispered soothingly to the dog, "You're safe now, buddy."

Chapter Twelve

Emily held the thermos cap down for the German Shepherd to lap at the small bit of water, but he turned his head away. Now that he was safe, he seemed at peace, but also like he was ready to take his last breath and just rest permanently. He was so skinny that it felt like he weighed less than Daisy.

As they drove, she tried to examine him without moving him around much. She could see part of one of his front foot pads was torn off and bleeding underneath. She could count every rib on him, and he smelled horrible. She spotted a flea near the corner of his eye.

With her phone, she'd found a vet clinic that was open 24 hours, and they headed there before doing anything else. Emily would've loved to take the dog to Dr. Sawyer back in Dragonfly Cove, but they weren't sure the dog had that much time.

"I wanted to break that fool's neck," Kuno said, his knuckles white on the steering wheel. "If we were in my town, I'd have slapped the handcuffs on him so fast his head would still be spinning."

She knew how he felt. She felt the same way.

"At least you saved one dog," she said. "And, hopefully, we can get the rest out of there."

He glanced over at her, then reached out and cradled the dog's muzzle in his big hand. "Yeah. Hopefully. But I've been a part of this kind of situation before. Right now, Ronald is calling in the troops. Every friend he ever had—and first cousins twice removed—offering them money to come help him clean up. He'll hide the sickest of the dogs and do what he can to meet the lowest of requirements to keep his certification. He could get off with a slap on the wrist despite what we saw."

"Even if the state finds out that they were a breeder who got their USDA license revoked and immediately applied as a 501(c)(3) rescue? Working from the same address?"

He shrugged. "Sometimes, yeah. It's not fair, but putting out these backyard breeders is like playing Whac-A-Mole. They always find a way to pop back up and continue doing business. Just look at the thousands of rescues online. If you keep seeing them post photos of full breed puppies, that's a red flag. Facebook has given them a whole new platform to sell from, calling it rescue. You and I both know, to get puppies into an official rescue is unusual, unless they are mutts. Not that there's anything wrong with a mutt. Hell, some of my best childhood dogs were mutts. They get a bad rap."

She could see a tic in his clenched jaw as he talked, telling her that he was doing his best to hide just how angry he was. "What's the next step?" she asked. "We must do something. I won't be able to live with myself if we don't."

"Oh, I'm going to do something, alright. For starters, when we get to the clinic and get this fellow settled, I'm calling the Department of Agriculture Protection Division."

"There it is," Emily said, pointing to the clinic. "North-side Animal Hospital."

Kuno pulled into a parking space and cut the motor, then jumped out and came around to her door. He opened it and carefully reached in and picked up the dog, blanket and all.

Emily jumped out after them and followed, then ran ahead and got the door.

The girl at the front desk took one look at the dog bundled up in Kuno's arms, then got up and beckoned for them to follow, peppering them with questions as she led them to a room and gestured for Kuno to lay the dog on the table.

When he did, the dog dropped his head heavily, letting it land on the stainless steel with a solid thump. His eyes were still open, and Emily held on to that, praying he could be saved.

Kuno shot Emily a warning look, then began answering what he could.

"We saw him from the road," he said. "He was lying down next to the tree line leading into some woods. I can't believe we noticed him."

The girl put her head out the door on the other side of the room.

"Need someone in Room B stat, please," she called out. "Emergency case."

A young woman in a white jacket strode quickly into the room. She pushed back her long, strawberry blonde hair and pulled her stethoscope off from around her neck.

"Hi, I'm Dr. Purvis," she said, then looked at the girl who led them into the room. "What do we have here, Savannah?"

"Stray. Found next to the highway. I haven't done

anything with him yet. I'm going to go get the intake forms. Be right back."

Dr. Purvis listened to the dog's chest, then pulled his eyelids open, looking closely. She shined her pen light in front of him, but he didn't follow her movements.

When Savannah returned, she turned to Emily and Kuno.

"Which one of you do I put down as the responsible party? We must have someone listed."

"Me, Kuno Fischer," he held his hand up. "But I live in Dragonfly Cove. I'd like to take him back there, if possible."

"He can't travel anywhere today," Dr. Purvis said. "We need to figure out what all is going on with this guy, and, by the looks of his vitals, he's going to need IV fluids all night, at the least. This paw needs to be debrided, and I want to get him in for x-rays, too. Savannah, do you have your scanner?"

The girl nodded and pulled a small tool from a cupboard behind them and handed it to the doctor. She began using it to slowly scan around the dog's shoulders in an S movement.

"What is that?" Kuno asked.

"This dog may have gotten lost," Dr. Purvis said, "We need to scan for a chip and see if we can find his owner. They may be looking for him. German Shepherds are valuable dogs."

Kuno exchanged worried glances with Emily.

Emily prayed under her breath that the Letons were too cheap to put microchips in their breeding dogs.

But that prayer went unanswered because the little machine beeped.

"Oh, that's great," Dr. Purvis said. "Now we can run the chip code through the registry to find the name and phone number of this dog's owner. Savannah, get Katy on that, then meet me in back. We've got to get moving on this boy before we lose him."

"Do you think he might not make it?" Emily asked, feeling weak with apprehension.

Dr. Purvis picked the dog up into her arms and turned to them.

"Look, I'm not going to give you false hope. This dog is in bad shape, and sometimes, once these kinds of cases get to safety, they just close their eyes and give up. Most of them don't have the courage to withstand the medical intervention to save them when they are this sick. I can try to stabilize him until we find the owners, but it could get costly if I find more to be done."

"I'll pay his bill," Kuno said.

"I'll help," Emily added, and Kuno immediately frowned at her and shook his head.

"Okay, that's kind of you both, considering it's not your dog. But if you want to spend the money, knowing he might not survive, I'll do what I can."

"Yes, do whatever it takes," Kuno said.

She nodded. "Go sit in the waiting room, and they'll get you all checked in and take a good-faith deposit. Then you might as well leave for a few hours until I see what we've got to deal with here."

Emily reached out and rubbed the dog's head. She fought back tears as she stepped back and let Kuno get closer to the dog.

"Listen, man," Kuno said, rubbing the dog's ear softly. "You be brave for me, okay? Get through this and I'll find you the best home in the world where you never want for anything again."

"Oh, one more thing," Dr. Purvis said. "We need a

name, at least until we reach the owners and find out what they call him."

Emily looked at Kuno and nodded, letting him know it was up to him.

"Valor," Kuno said. "I want to name him Valor."

Chapter Thirteen

Back in the truck, they sat in the parking lot. Kuno called the Department of Agriculture for Georgia, and was immediately told they didn't investigate on a local level, but they would take their complaint and then turn it over to the local animal control or law enforcement division.

"If that's the case, I'll call them directly," Kuno said into the phone, then hung up.

Emily was already searching for the number.

"It's under Valdosta Animal Services," she said. "Want me to call?"

He nodded and she dialed.

A man answered, claiming to be an Animal Control Officer. Emily explained their issue and he directed her to call up to the Admin building to file an official complaint for something of that magnitude. He rattled off the number, and Emily tried to keep it in her head.

She hung up and dialed again.

A voice mail picked up and said the person they were

trying to reach was on vacation, to leave a message and someone would get back to them soon.

"I can't believe this," Emily said. "It's a circle of madness."

"Right? What do they do in emergencies? Just play phone tag?"

"I'm contacting Jimmy." Kuno sent off a text to his buddy in the Valdosta Sheriff's Department.

"You think you can trust this deputy not to throw you under the bus about us going in there under false pretenses?" Emily asked worriedly. "I wouldn't want you to lose your job because of something I got you into."

"He won't throw me under. In this field, we don't betray each other."

"Good," she said, nodding. That was one less thing to worry about. She was glad he knew a sheriff's deputy in the area. "What about the microchip? If it comes up with their names, what are we going to do to keep them from taking Valor back?"

He leaned back and ran his hands through his thick, black hair.

"I don't know. I'm thinking." Then he turned to her. "It's all about the timing. If we can get the sheriff's department over there stat, they'll get Animal Services involved. It'll be chaotic, and claiming Valor will be the last thing they'll want to do."

"You have a point there," Emily said. "If they claim him, they'll have to take responsibility for the shape he's in. Maybe we'll get lucky, and they'll say he's not theirs."

"But we also need to use his case against them," Kuno said. He sighed loudly. "Let's just wait and talk to Jimmy."

It was well past lunch time now and Emily didn't want to say anything about being hungry, considering there were more important things afoot than her stomach, but it suddenly betrayed her, growling loudly.

Kuno looked over at her, and she felt her checks flush.

"That coffee this morning didn't go far, did it?" he asked.

She smiled wryly. "I usually eat at noon, and my system knows it."

"I can take care of that," he said. "The vet said don't come back for a few hours, so I'll get Jimmy to meet us somewhere. His choice since we don't know the area."

He took his phone from his shirt pocket and texted furiously.

A text came back immediately.

Kuno read it, then handed his phone to Emily.

> Rico's Tacos. 250 N St Augustine. Order through the drive through then grab an outside table. I want 3 carne asada tacos. Meet you there in 15.

Emily clicked the address.

"Go left out of here," she said, directing him out of the parking lot, her mouth still watering from reading about tacos. "So how do you know Jimmy?"

Kuno's gaze wandered the streets ahead as he reminisced, "Let's see ... the first time I met Jimmy was during a highly confidential joint operation that brought together our respective law enforcement departments across both Florida and Georgia. Jimmy was in the same role for his side. We were all staying at the same cheap motel. You know the kind that you walk out the door and you're in the parking lot? His room was beside mine and we connected over a beer one evening, talking about our boredom while we sat on my truck bed."

"Sounds like a fun experience," she said.

"Yeah. I like stuff like that. Anyway, Jimmy and I spent some time talking about his heritage, which was really evident by his appearance. He told me that Valdosta, his hometown, was first settled by the Creek and Seminole Indians, then Spanish missionaries before American pioneers took over. He's got six generations of family who have made this area their home."

Intrigued, Emily leaned in and prodded for more, "That's so interesting. Did you ever find out more about what was so confidential?"

He laughed. "If I did, I couldn't tell you."

She punched him playfully in the arm. "Jeez. I thought we were going to have some noteworthy conversation."

He struck himself in the heart, as though he'd been stabbed. "Ouch. Is my conversation not interesting enough for you thus far?"

"Well, I loved the part about Jimmy's heritage, but you had me on the hook about the joint operation. My writer's curiosity is piqued. Way to leave me dangling," she said, grinning at him.

"Okay, I'll tell you this much. Some things went down to shake up our boredom in that case. Rocked me to my boots, but Jimmy never wavered. He was a rock—proved himself to be someone you could always count on, no matter how dire the circumstances."

Nodding in understanding, Emily encouraged him to continue, "So, what happened afterward? How did you two stay connected?"

Kuno wore a nostalgic smile as he continued, "Well, you see, after that operation, we both realized the incredible value of having a connection like that—someone you could trust implicitly. So, we made sure to stay in touch, even though he's stationed here in Georgia, and I'm down in Florida. We've visited each other a few times."

"Oh, here it is," Emily pointed.

As they pulled their truck into the parking lot of an old, weathered building—the sign out front proclaimed 'Drive-Thru Only'—Emily's anticipation continued to mount. With the tacos ordered, they parked and grabbed an available outdoor table, basking in the warmth of the balmy spring Georgia afternoon. The air was filled with the enticing aroma of sizzling, grilled meat, making her hunger even more palpable.

Their wait was brief, and a tall, friendly-looking man soon approached their table. Jimmy looked like he was mid-40s, and he exuded a welcoming presence. With his noble, Native American profile and his hair slicked back in a neat ponytail, he wore his dark gray sheriff's deputy uniform with a sense of authority that made it clear he was every bit the dedicated officer. Emily thought it amusing that his favorite food was of Mexican cuisine.

"Kuno!" he called, then stuck his hand out.

Kuno jumped to his feet, and they exchanged a complicated handshake that ended in a fist bump and both clasping each other around the shoulder before retreating.

Emily was struck by Jimmy's warm and approachable demeanor, despite what first appeared to be a stern countenance.

"This is Emily," Kuno said.

"Nice to meet you, ma'am," Jimmy said, shaking her hand gently.

They all sat down, and she passed out the food and three bottles of water.

Jimmy looked from Kuno to Emily.

"How long have you two been dating?" he asked.

"Oh, no. We're just friends," Emily said, feeling her cheeks flush.

Kuno raised his eyebrows at her and smiled.

"Yep. Friends on a mission," he added.

They began eating, and their conversation quickly delved into the heart of the matter—the shocking discovery of the supposed "dog rescue" facility that had turned out to be no more than a grim puppy mill.

Jimmy put his last taco down to listen closer.

Kuno's voice carried the weight of what they had witnessed. "Jimmy, you wouldn't believe it. The place was a living nightmare. Dogs crammed into tiny cages, some of them visibly sick and emaciated. There was filth everywhere, and the stench was overpowering."

"Sounds like a bust we did on another puppy mill here a few years ago," Jimmy said., shaking his head.

"And, man, I hate to tell you this, but we took a dog," Kuno said, bending his head toward Jimmy and lowering his voice.

Jimmy looked alarmed.

Emily's eyes filled with emotion as she quickly added, "It was an adult German Shepherd, and he looked like he was dying. His fur was matted, and he was trembling. He was clearly injured and starving, too. We couldn't just leave him there."

Jimmy listened intently, his expression shifting from curiosity to deep concern. It was evident that he grasped the severity of the situation. His furrowed brow conveyed a growing unease.

"That might be complicated," Jimmy said with a sigh. "Taking someone else's dog without permission, that could be considered theft. We should've sent Animal Control out there for him."

"We've since called them. It was round robin on the phone. Even if they had answered, we all know how long it takes to get Animal Control to a scene," Kuno said. "This dog didn't have time to waste."

"He might not even make it," Emily said sadly.

She felt uneasy. The gravity of their actions was beginning to sink in, and the potential legal repercussions of their impulsive rescue mission nearly made her regret their actions. But, no, if she had to face arrest for what they'd done, so be it.

"So, what do you think?" Kuno asked him after a tense silence settled around them.

Jimmy sighed deeply. He looked at his watch. "I have to get back to the department and check in. Send me the photos you have. I'll ask my sergeant about this and see what we can do, but I have a feeling that, with us being so busy, he's going to punt it to the Animal Control as first on scene. Maybe Georgia Department of Agriculture."

"We've already called them, too. They stated to contact our local animal control or sheriff's department," Kuno said. "It's a crazy circle of getting nowhere."

"Okay, then, yeah—Sarge will have a direct contact at animal control."

Kuno looked relieved. "Thanks for whatever you can do, Jimmy. Keep in touch with any feedback. We'll head back to the clinic and check on Valor."

"Oh, shit," Jimmy said.

"What?" Kuno looked alarmed.

"You went and named him, didn't you? You know what that means." He gave a sardonic grin and shook his head. "Talk at you later. Emily, nice meeting you. You take care now, you hear?"

Chapter Fourteen

They hadn't been gone quite two hours, but the second they walked back into the clinic they were shown to a room by a grim-looking young woman who introduced herself as Lexi, the Patient Care Director.

"Wait here for Dr. Purvis," she said, shutting the door softly as she disappeared back into the medical side of the building.

Emily tried to keep the panic out of her eyes. "He died, didn't he? She won't tell us because it's the doctor's duty to give the bad news."

"We don't know that, Emily. Stay positive," Kuno said, pacing the small room nervously.

"I could see it in her eyes. Hear it in her voice."

Emily took the only chair, other than the doctor's stool.

Kuno stopped in front of her.

"If he dies, that's more ammunition against them, but let's pray he didn't."

She nodded, swallowing hard past the lump in her throat.

Fifteen excruciatingly long minutes later, Dr. Purvis came in, carrying a folder as she took a seat on her stool.

"Okay, he's on IV treatment and holding his own, but we aren't out of the woods yet," she said.

Emily and Kuno collectively breathed a sigh of relief.

Dr. Purvis continued. "First, he's not as old as he looks. He's six years old with the current prowess of a dog twice his age. Malnourished, obviously. He's at thirty pounds and should be at around sixty-five, at least. He's got a nasty infection on one paw, anemic probably from flea infestation, and he needs a handful of rotted teeth extracted. To be honest, he's full of parasites and, unfortunately, he's also heart worm positive."

When she stopped, Emily was feeling sick.

Poor Valor. That was a lot to overcome.

"Aren't heart worms fatal in dogs?" Kuno asked.

"Not always," Dr. Purvis said. "His case will be very delicate, though. We give a 3-part injection that will kill 98% of the adult worms. What will be the most important is that he does nothing but rest as he recovers. If he strains at all, he could be in danger of pulmonary embolisms due to the dying worms blocking his lungs from adequate blood flow."

Emily felt gutted even more.

"And that could be instantaneously fatal."

Emily thought of the microchip and hoped the doctor had forgotten.

"And about that microchip," Dr. Purvis continued, then opened her folder. "His official name is Cash."

Ironic. Or maybe not, considering that was the only reason the Letons had him: to bring in cash for his puppies.

"Yes, about that," Emily said, desperately trying to think of what to say.

"Just listen to this first," the doctor said, looking at them gravely as she began to read from a paper in her folder. "Puppy FebA, brought in by Lori Louise Leton. Positive for Parvo and placed under quarantine via state law. Died a week later. A week after that, Puppy FebB and Puppy FebC brought in, and both died. None of the three ever had the courtesy of real names, and their ashes were not requested to be returned."

She looked up solemnly.

Kuno started to say something, but she held her hand up for him to stop.

"No dogs brought in for another six months, then a very old Yorkshire terrier mama with an emergency caesarean. I was able to save two of the four. The dog looked overbred and was too old to have any more litters. I told just that to Ms. Lori Louise Leton, the owner of the dog you brought in today who is back there fighting for his life. And that is why, if he survives, I will be deactivating his microchip, and releasing him either into your care, or to a dog rescue that I work closely with. Of course, I'll need your discretion and permission."

She locked eyes with Emily, then Kuno.

"That woman is a monster," she whispered. "She's been shut down, but any of her dogs that fall into my lap won't be returning to hers. As far as I'm concerned, your dog is not Cash. He's Valor, a stray dog without identification or a microchip."

"We totally agree, and, yes, we will keep his identity between us, but we have bad news," Kuno said. "She's still breeding and selling dogs. Some of them to the pet store in our town in Florida. We've tracked her and witnessed her facility today. It's horrific."

The doctor looked disgusted. "Can't say I'm surprised.

They always find a way to circumvent the law. I can help with that, but my immediate question to you is what do you want to do with Valor?"

Emily looked at Kuno.

She couldn't take another dog. She could barely handle Daisy.

He didn't even hesitate.

"Get him stable enough for a three-hour road trip, and I'll be taking him home and straight to Emily's veterinarian. As of this minute, Valor is my family, and family is something I take very seriously."

Emily felt relief wash through her.

"Good," said Dr. Purvis. "But he can't travel today. I can check his white blood cell count in the morning and, if he's improved at all, I can hook up a portable IV in your vehicle, if you promise you will indeed take him straight to your veterinarian."

Kuno held his hand up and crossed it over his heart.

"Scout's honor," he said. "And thank you. For everything."

Chapter Fifteen

The man behind the counter of the McKey Hotel in downtown Valdosta was oblivious to Emily's discomfort as he handed over the key to the room called "Gypsy's Last Parade." His name tag said *Maurice*, but he looked more like a Mac or a Grover. He was dressed very neatly and professionally, but something in his accent and mannerisms wanted her to put him in an episode of Andy Griffith, rather than the posh boutique hotel he managed.

"You're lucky that we had a last-minute cancellation," he said cheerfully. "With every room in town booked months in advance for the Georgia Annual Film Festival, a room doesn't usually come open this week. Poor Mr. and Mrs. Higginbotham from Atlanta secured their reservation more than a year ago. It's her favorite room, because of the elephant theme, I guess. She gives to the elephant rescues in South Asia, or something like that."

"I see," Kuno said, plopping his credit card down on the counter. "That's very nice of her."

Emily hid her smile.

Kuno wasn't the type to chat on and on.

Maurice continued. "The Higginbothams had quite a morning. I'm sure we'll see it on the news later. They had to make an emergency landing with their private helicopter, and Mrs. Higginbotham was so shaken up that she wanted to go back home. Mr. Higginbotham—he's the director of that famous movie called *Charlibet*; you know the one ... it's about a woman whose husband leaves her after she is disfigured in an accident. She goes back to her hometown to find her first love, who doesn't recognize her, and —well, I'm sure you saw it. Anyway, Mr. Higginbotham decided to rest up and drive in tomorrow. He doesn't know I'm giving his room up, so you'll have to be out by checkout time, no dallying around. Just in case he comes a bit earlier than usual."

As far as Emily could tell, Maurice hadn't taken a breath during that whole monologue. It was quite extraordinary.

"That won't be a problem," Kuno said.

Emily could see his body language was saying he wished the man would just finish the check-in procedure.

Maurice paused to focus on keying in the information from Kuno's driver's license.

They'd decided to stay in Valdosta until the next day when they could hopefully take Valor home with them. No sense in driving it all twice when Mari said she was happy enough to stay overnight at Emily's to take care of Daisy.

After all, Emily was exhausted and, though Kuno wouldn't admit it, he was, too. It had been a long and stressful day, and all she wanted was a bath and somewhere to stretch out. Driving three hours to get it wasn't appealing.

Unfortunately, they'd struck out on finding two rooms available at any hotel.

"I swear, I'll be a perfect gentleman," Kuno had whispered to her in the lobby, urging her to share the room.

Going against her better judgment, she'd agreed.

"After next week, there won't be a front desk," Maurice said.

"Oh? The hotel is closing?" Kuno asked.

Maurice laughed. "Heavens, no. We're going contactless. It will be just like Airbnb, where you check in online and have a code to get into your room. I'm here now because, during big city events, the owners like to have a personal touch. And, to be honest, I enjoy going back to the old way for a bit. I'm a people person."

The *old* way.

That was disturbing. Emily didn't know that hotels were starting to go contactless. It felt strange to think that, one day, public lodging wouldn't have front desks or key cards. No face-to-face customer service? It sounded awful, and she hoped it didn't come to that while she was alive. The world was moving too fast for her as it was.

"Okay, all done," he said, sliding a piece of paper toward Kuno. "Here's your door code. Would you like someone to carry your luggage up? Mac is there this week for that, too. He's usually just the custodian."

So, there *was* a Mac!

Emily felt a bit vindicated.

"No, thank you." Kuno said, picking up the slip of paper. "We'll manage."

He didn't tell Maurice that they didn't have any luggage.

"Is there a Walmart close to here?" Emily asked.

Maurice nodded. "Honey, just take your pick. We've got several Walmarts around town. You can't swing a dead cat without hitting one."

"Okay, thank you." The *swinging cat* adage was a bit gruesome—as well as a first for her—but she was glad a Walmart run would be convenient. She wanted to pick up something comfortable to sleep in, as well as some toiletries. It was going to be awkward enough without having to sleep in her clothes and wear them the next day. Not to mention, she felt like she still smelled of puppy mill and looked forward to getting the scent off her.

Maurice stood back and smiled. "Have a great evening, Mr. and Mrs. Fischer."

Emily looked at Kuno, and he gave her a cheesy grin, holding up the paper.

"C'mon, *honey*. Let's go see our room."

Chapter Sixteen

E mily and Kuno made their way to the fourth floor, curious to see the room called "Gypsy's Last Parade." Emily had expected to see bold, safari wallpaper and portraits of elephants, given the name of the room, but she was in for a surprise. As they entered, they were greeted by a modern black and white design that was a far cry from any jungle motif.

"Nice," Kuno said, whistling through his teeth softly.

Emily went straight to the window, drawn by the view of downtown Valdosta. She gazed out at the cityscape. The view was surprisingly pleasant, and it helped ease her earlier discomfort. However, her tranquility was short-lived when she realized that there was only one bed in the room. King-sized, but still—only one bed.

"Um ..." She turned to Kuno, her eyebrows raised in surprise.

He caught her reaction and quickly assured her, "I'll go down and ask for more bedding and sleep on the floor."

She nodded, appreciating his consideration. "That sounds like a plan. They should have some soft duvets they can loan you. We can stop by when we come back in from dinner."

After checking out the bathroom, and exclaiming over the free toiletries of shampoo, soap, and lotion, they headed downstairs and out to the truck.

"Walmart first?" she asked.

She wanted to buy pajamas and something to wear for the next day. The thought of sleeping in her current clothes, still carrying the faint odor of the puppy mill, wasn't appealing.

As Maurice had stated, there was a Walmart just a few miles away. A quick run through the store—Emily grabbing black leggings, sweatshirt, socks, and underwear, and Kuno stocking up on snacks—and they were back in the truck.

"Now where?" he said, looking at her.

She shrugged. "Too early for dinner. You choose."

He started the engine. "Let's just see what we see."

They drove around for a bit before stumbling on the Valdosta Museum, and they agreed it would be a good place to waste some time.

Inside, Kuno was immediately drawn to a Civil War exhibit in recognition of the war's sesquicentennial. While he immersed himself in the historical artifacts, Emily found herself captivated by another exhibit.

Ole Maurice wasn't kidding. There really was a famous elephant named Gypsy!

She looked at the black and white photos and read through the posted information, absorbing the history of Gypsy, the large Asian elephant who had once belonged to the Harris's Nickel Plate circus. The story detailed how Gypsy had killed her trainer in Valdosta in 1902, going on a rampage through town before being subdued by gunfire by the chief of police. The incident had been so peculiar that people from surrounding towns had accused Valdosta of fabricating the story for publicity. Luckily there was a photographer around for proof, though the pictures were grainy.

"What's this?" Kuno asked, coming up beside her.

"Our hotel room's namesake."

He read a bit, then chuckled. "Come on. A circus travels all over the world. Why would they keep the elephant in Valdosta?"

Emily pointed at one of the posters. "It says the circus chose Valdosta for their winter quarters because of the fairgrounds' suitability and the year-round mild weather."

"So sad," Kuno said. "Killed because she dared to try to escape her captivity."

"That's why I never go to a circus," Emily said.

"Same. I despise the whole idea. It's barbaric."

After finishing reading, she couldn't help but feel a sense of connection to the poor elephant named Gypsy, but also to the city's history, even if it involved a tragic event.

Kuno had moved on, and she rejoined him where he was engrossed in an exhibit of the Moody Air Force Base. Emily wasn't interested in aviation, but it was fascinating that George W. Bush was noted as having completed his flight training there and had even dated a Valdosta State College cheerleader while he was in town.

"I wonder if Laura knew about that," she joked to Kuno.

They finished up at the museum and returned to the hotel to get cleaned up. Emily was first to shower, and it felt so good to let the hot water fall over her and wash away the remnants of the puppy mill. Even so, she couldn't stop thinking of Valor, and said a prayer for him, urging him to keep fighting. If he didn't make it through the night, Emily had a feeling that Kuno would be devastated.

Once she was out, Kuno went in to take his turn.

She took the free minutes to touch base with Mari again, who said she was currently under a mound of covers on Emily's bed, watching Netflix and eating her ice cream. Daisy beside her.

"She has to sleep in her crate, Mari," Emily scolded.

Mari promised that, once the movie was over, she'd take Daisy out again and then put her to bed. Emily wasn't so sure, and, if Daisy ruined another rug, Mari was going to hear about it.

Quickly, Emily gave Mari the highlights of what they'd seen inside the dog rescue, and promised to fill her in more when she got home, before hanging up and perusing her inbox on her phone.

There were three emails marked urgent, from the fitness trainer she was writing the book for, wanting to know where the latest chapter was.

Emily wanted to throw her phone.

She was so sick of writing about vegetables and, anyway, it was only two days late! Her clients could be so demanding. They thought they were creating the next *To Kill A Mockingbird.*

Kuno emerged from the bathroom—showered and smelling delicious. He'd changed into a spare uniform he kept in his truck and looked spiffy.

"Did you buy cologne?" she asked.

"Just some cheap body spray," he said, then picked up his wallet and keys.

It didn't smell cheap to her.

"Oh, I almost forgot," he said, pulling a small bag from his pocket and handing it to her. "I got you this."

"What is it?"

"Just a little something to remember today, our first outing together."

It wasn't a Walmart bag. Where else did he go that she didn't know about? She looked in the bag to find a small velvet box. She pulled it out and opened the top to find a charming silver bracelet. She looked closer and saw a tiny, silver elephant pendant hanging from it.

"Kuno, this is so nice! It's supposed to be Gypsy, isn't it?"

He nodded, but was suddenly shy. "Yep. Just a friendship bracelet. I found it in the museum gift shop and thought you'd like it."

She smiled up at him. "You're wrong. I don't like it. I love it."

He grinned back. "Good."

"Thank you so much, Kuno. It was very thoughtful of you. Will you help me put it on?"

When he'd hooked it around her wrist, he held the door, and they went down to the lobby, then left the hotel, walking in search of somewhere to eat dinner.

"This looks nice," Kuno said when they came upon a restaurant named 306 *North*.

Emily peered through the window and grimaced. "Too nice. It even has tablecloths. But you look handsome in your uniform and I'm wearing workout attire from Walmart. I can't go in there like this."

He made a funny expression and put his hand over his heart playfully. "Oh ... I look *handsome*, huh? Maybe you *like* me ..."

She blushed. "Stop it. You know what I mean. Next to you in your clean uniform, I'll look like a criminal that you're transporting to the local jail."

"Not quite, but don't worry about it," he said. "You look great, and no one knows us here, anyway. Come on, Emily. It's either this or McDonald's. Do you really want greasy burgers and fries after we've already pigged out on tacos today?"

He had a point.

Her hips sure didn't need any more fast food.

The aromas coming from the place convinced her that he (and her hips) was right, and they went in and were immediately seated at a table in the corner. It was next to the windows, and they could watch people walking by.

They perused the menu and decided to order shrimp and grits with a side of roasted okra. Kuno said he would order for them both, and he did, proving to be very smooth with the server. She barely looked old enough to drink, but she was obviously enamored with a man in uniform. She flirted with Kuno a bit, and he didn't take the bait, so she hurried away, promising to return with their drinks and bread.

"She was interested," Emily teased.

"Too young. I like my woman seasoned," he joked back.

The girl returned and put down the drinks and bread, looked Kuno straight in the eye while ignoring Emily, and told him to let her know if he needed anything else.

As they waited for their dinner, they engaged in small talk.

Emily fiddled with the elephant on her bracelet.

Outside the window, a couple had stopped and were arguing. The woman was pointing at the phone her partner held in his hand, and she appeared to be angry.

"She saw a text message from someone else," Kuno said, wagging his eyebrows at her.

"Or she's mad because he's supposed to be giving her

attention, instead of checking his social media. She's telling him it's either TikTok or her, to make his choice."

Kuno laughed as the woman threw her arms across her chest and stomped off.

"Now he's trying to figure out whether he should chase her or go find a bar to have a few tall beers in," Emily whispered.

The man followed the woman, looking frustrated.

"Nope, he's going to try to salvage the night," Kuno added. "I bet a nickel he can't find her now. She's slipped into a public restroom somewhere and is going to hide out until he's really sweating it."

"That's really sad, actually. What a waste of a beautiful night that they can never get back. My grandma used to say that love is not running or giving up, that it's staying and fighting for every single moment you have together."

"I like that," he said. "And I totally agree."

With the couple gone, and no more interesting parties going by on the street, Emily tried to think of something else to say.

"I was just thinking about the hotel situation and how we couldn't find two rooms. I never knew there were movie festivals, or that any movies were even made in Georgia," she admitted.

Kuno, obviously a movie buff, held his hand over his chest and feigned shock.

"You didn't know that some of the *Marvel* superhero movies have been filmed in and around Atlanta? *Ant Man*, *The Avengers*, and even *Captain America* and *Spiderman-Homecoming*."

She laughed. "Sorry—I can't say I'm into superhero stuff."

He sat back in his chair dramatically. "Fine. But what

about classics like *Smokey and the Bandit*, and *My Cousin Vinny*? Heck, even scenes from *The Walking Dead* were filmed near Atlanta."

Emily burst into laughter at the look on his face. "I'm a reader, Kuno! But, yes, you can relax a little because I've seen parts of *Smokey and the Bandit*. My dad is a huge fan of Burt Reynolds. I think he's seen all his movies at least a dozen or more times and made me sit through half of them."

"Thank you, Jesus, for a good dad," he said, sighing in relief. "I thought we were going to have to go back and have a movie marathon tonight, and I'm too tired for that."

"Same." She picked at her shrimp, feeling self-conscious again at the mention of returning to the hotel. She didn't relish the getting-into-bed part. Especially since she was the only one who would be doing it.

Too bad the floor in their room wasn't carpeted.

It was going to be a long night for Kuno.

She had to admit, she was learning a lot about him. So far, she knew he was loyal to friends, had a soft spot for the underdog, and had little boy taste when it came to the big screen.

Oh, and he was such a gentleman.

A *very sexy gentleman*, at that.

She looked down at her bracelet. So lovely, but a gift wasn't any reason to let a man sleep in your bed, she told herself sternly. That would be like going home with someone from a bar just because they bought you a drink.

Something she would never do. She had more class than that.

However, Kuno wouldn't even be on this crazy trip and would be home in his comfortable own bed if it wasn't for her getting him involved. Even jeopardizing his job.

A shotgun aimed at him, too!

"Would you like dessert?" he asked.

"God, no. I'm so full I'll probably have to waddle back to the hotel."

He chuckled. "I doubt that, but okay. I'll get the check."

He began to look around the restaurant for their server.

"Kuno," she said, getting his attention.

He turned back to her and raised his eyebrows inquiringly. "Yes? Decide to take me up on dessert?"

"No. But I did change my mind about one thing. You can sleep in the bed, too. I'm not going to make you stay on the hard floor after the day we've had."

He smiled broadly. "Glad you said that, Emily. I was actually going to camp out in my truck. That floor looks none too inviting. But tell you what—I'll build the best pillow wall between us that you've ever seen. I promise not to try anything, and you won't even know I'm there. Like you said, we're just friends. Deal?"

She smiled, doubting that it would be possible to forget his presence so close to her. But he didn't need to know that.

"Deal."

Chapter Seventeen

S unday morning arrived, and Emily turned off the highway onto Victor Drive. After a restless night with Kuno sleeping just inches away, they had risen early and grabbed a quick coffee and sausage biscuit from Hardee's before continuing their journey to Dragonfly Cove with Valor in tow.

Their pillow wall hadn't survived the night, but their oath to only be friends did. Kuno hadn't tried to make a move on her. Part of Emily was glad that he'd stood by his promise. The other part was a bit disappointed, if she was being totally honest.

Kuno's phone signaled a text and he read it, then turned to her.

"Operation Valor," he said, smiling widely.

"What do you mean?"

"I mean, Jimmy has good news. The photos were enough that they're going to plan a task force to go into the Leton's facility. They're calling it *Operation Valor*. It's going to take a few weeks to coordinate, though. Law enforcement will accompany animal control and the local Humane Society, along with members of a real rescue they're familiar with to help disburse the dogs they seize and get them to safety."

"That's fantastic news!"

He nodded and then sent off a reply.

"I told him I want to be a part of it. He's going to ask his sergeant if I can help. But, Emily, I'm sorry, you and Mari can't go. They won't want civilians involved unless it's in a professional capacity."

"I understand. It's enough that it's going to happen, whether I'm there to see it or not. I'm going to start working on getting Dogland to stop buying from puppy mills. They need to know where some of their pups are really coming from."

"They probably don't want to know," Kuno said. "All they see is money. Buy them for a couple hundred each, sell them for a couple thousand. That's quite a markup, even if some dogs die in the transition. It's an evil enterprise just to line the pockets of greedy people all through the pipeline. And Dogland pet store shouldn't be off the hook, either. Someone had to know something was up with the Letons."

He was right, and it was disturbing how greed could cause such havoc to living things. She didn't have anything against proper dog breeders. Ones like Leslie who took good care of their dogs and weren't in it to be rich. Professional breeders treat their sires and bitches like family, retiring them when they'd had just a few litters. Some of them were adopted out to lovers of the breed, and others stayed with her through their golden years.

None were stuck out in a chicken coop, rejected and neglected, like Valor.

But something Kuno said about Dogland not being off the hook gave her an idea. She might not be able to be there when they brought down Ronald and his mother, Lori Leton, but that didn't mean there was nothing Emily could do to help. She needed to think on it more before she brought it up to Kuno.

"Hey—we're close to the clinic now," she said, seeing the clinic's sign coming up. "Two minutes out. Dr. Sawyer should be there waiting for us."

She had called Dr. Sawyer, her veterinarian, before leaving Georgia, explaining the situation and Kuno's desire for Valor to receive treatment close to home. Dr. Sawyer didn't usually work on Sunday, but, in this case, he'd agreed to meet them and set Valor up in their intensive care unit. He requested all the documentation from Northside but emphasized that he needed to conduct his own examination before starting any treatment for the heart worms, as Valor's condition was critical.

Dr. Purvis had rigged an IV and given Valor a sedative to keep him calm during the journey. Kuno decided to let Emily drive so that he could hold the precious dog in his arms. He mentioned that it was to ensure Valor remained still, but Emily suspected there was more to it. Kuno looked like a gentle giant, constantly soothing Valor with gentle strokes to his ear and forehead.

"I can't wait to stretch my legs," Kuno said. "I'm so stiff from not moving, but I didn't want to wake him."

When Valor had settled onto Kuno's lap, he'd stared up at Kuno for the longest time, but then fell asleep and hadn't stirred for at least a few hours. It was as though he knew that he was safe and could let his guard down.

Either that, or he was so sick he couldn't do anything but close his eyes.

"You'll love Dr. Sawyer," she said. "He's no nonsense. Tells it like it is."

"My kind of guy," Kuno replied.

Upon arriving at Bayshore Veterinary Clinic, Emily followed Kuno inside as he carried Valor. They were promptly shown to a room, where they put Valor on the exam table and patiently awaited Dr. Sawyer's arrival.

Valor was awake now and was trembling with confusion.

Dr. Sawyer entered the room.

"Emily," he said, nodding in acknowledgement. "Good to see you."

"Thanks, Dr. Sawyer. This is my friend Kuno Fischer."

The men shook hands and the doctor immediately got to work examining Valor. Then he flipped through the documentation from Northside Clinic, reading it quickly.

He turned to them. "I agree with Dr. Purvis' assessment," he began, his voice gentle. "Valor is still in a critical condition, and it could go either way at this point. We'll get him set up in our intensive care unit, and we'll monitor him round the clock."

"When can I see him again?" Kuno asked, deep furrows creasing his forehead.

"You can call and check on his progress in the morning."

Kuno left a deposit with the front desk clerk to cover Valor's treatment, his worry etched across his face. As they left the clinic, he took the wheel, his expression a mix of sadness and concern.

Emily hated seeing him look so discouraged.

She reached over and patted his arm, offering reassurance. "We're doing everything we can for Valor, Kuno. He's in good hands now."

"I know," Kuno said. "I just can't stop thinking about how many years he spent being abused and neglected, living in that tiny, wire coop except when they needed him to perform. It takes a sick, twisted mind to put a dog through that kind of life. I want to see them go to jail. Not just for Valor, but for all the dogs they've mistreated."

"I do, too," she said softly.

Kuno pulled up in front of Emily's house, his mood obviously still heavy. "Thank you, Emily, for everything."

She smiled softly and asked, "Why are you thanking me? I'm the one who is grateful. Do you want to come in for a bit? You could use some rest."

He shook his head, sighing. "I've got to get home, check on things, and get ready for work tomorrow."

Emily nodded, understanding the weight of his responsibilities. "Alright, Kuno. Take care of yourself, and we'll keep in touch about Valor."

As Kuno drove away, Emily watched him go. She couldn't help but worry about him.

When he was out of sight, she went inside.

"There you are," Mari exclaimed. "I thought maybe you ran away with Deputy McDreamie."

"Funny," Emily said. "Where's Daisy?"

"I just let her out in the backyard. She's been restless today. Missing you, I think."

They went through the kitchen to the back door and Emily stepped out first.

Daisy was busy trying to dig up a very young rose bush.

"No, Daisy," Emily shouted. "Don't kill my roses!"

Hearing her voice, Daisy turned and looked, and her little face was transformed to pure joy. She galloped over and—dirty paws and all—jumped up on Emily.

She barked and rubbed her head on Emily's legs in a joyful Labrador-type hug, then began a round of zoomies around the yard.

Emily and Mari laughed. Daisy was a sight.

"I guess she missed me," Emily said.

"You think?" Mari deadpanned.

"Now, let's go in and you can tell me everything. Starting with where you slept and where he slept, if he made a move, then all about the dog facility."

"You're silly," Emily said. But she was glad that Mari was there, being a friend that Emily could depend on.

Chapter Eighteen

Monday was chaos and Tuesday was looking like Emily might have some breathing room for a few hours before she had to go to work as soon as her company left.

"Why can't we be there?" Mari asked.

"We've already gone over this. We're civilians and, because they already know Ronald has weapons and isn't afraid to brandish them, it's too dangerous. Kuno has promised to keep us aware of each step along the way. After all, if it wasn't for you, none of this would be happening, so you can feel good in knowing that you started the process."

She looked downcast. "Yeah, but I feel bad for being a part of the puppy mill pipeline in the first place."

"Hey—look at me," Emily said, going to sit next to Mari on the couch. "When you know better, you do better. You had no idea where Ladybug came from, and it's a common misconception that pet stores only get their supply from reputable breeders."

They heard a knock at the door.

When she peeked out, she yelled, jolting Mari out of her funk.

"What is it?" Mari asked, coming to her feet quickly.

Emily threw the door open and held her arms out, and Leslie fell into them.

"Why didn't you tell me you were coming home?" Emily exclaimed when they finally released each other.

"Just wanted to surprise you," Leslie said.

She looked great. Tanned and even a bit thinner, or at least it looked like it in the sleek white linen outfit she wore, something Emily hadn't seen on her before.

"Look at you," she said, bowing at the waist. "My queen. You look positively radiant. All that loving looks good on you."

"Yeah—about that," Leslie said, her smile disappearing as she knelt in front of Daisy, kissing her on the nose while she ruffled her fur. "I might share but, first, wine. And how is this precious girl doing?"

"I'll get that wine before I tell you what a terror she is. Mari, this is Leslie. Mari, that's Daisy's real mom. Get acquainted," Emily said, going to the kitchen. Then she remembered that Mari wasn't quite old enough to drink just let. "Mari, what do you want to drink?"

"Dr. Pepper. No glass needed."

It didn't look like Emily was going to have time to catch up on the work she owed her current author. But Leslie took priority over a chapter titled "Carrots and Couches: The Two Can Coincide Peacefully." That's all she had so far because, to be honest, she hated carrots, so her muse was hiding. She also had much more important things on her mind than finding a way to convince readers that carrots were their friend.

When Emily returned with a bottle of Chardonnay, two

glasses, a can of Dr. Pepper and a plate of shortbread cookies, Mari was already laying out the story of Ladybug. She was at the part about Emily and Kuno finding out that it was a bad breeder posing as a rescue that had supplied the dog to the pet store.

"I'm so sorry about your puppy," Leslie said. "That's so tragic. But they wouldn't refund your money? I know Dogland charges a lot for their dogs."

Mari shook her head. "They stated I only had 48 hours to bring her back."

"But what about Florida's Pet Lemon Law? It still should've fallen under that."

Emily sat down just in time to catch Mari's bewildered look.

"What pet lemon law?" Emily asked as she handed Mari the can, then poured a healthy portion of wine in the glasses.

Leslie took one. "Under the statute, a pet dealer can be in a lot of trouble for selling a sick dog. When the purchase is made, they are representing the dog to you as healthy. If that proves not to be true, the buyer can return the animal for a refund or for a different dog. Or the dealer must pay medical costs if the buyer wishes to recover the dog."

"Hmm," Emily said. "The manager of Dogland didn't mention that. What's the time frame?"

"I had Ladybug for a week before she got sick," Mari said.

"Oh, that's kind of tricky," Leslie said. "The law states that the consumer must notify the pet dealer within two business days of a veterinarian's determination that the animal was unfit. And they have three days to provide the seller with written certification of the animal's unfitness."

"See, that's where they get you," Emily said. "In Ladybug's case, Mari didn't know she was that sick until after five days or so."

"Too bad it was an illness that took her, and not something congenital," Leslie said, sighing sadly.

"Wait," Emily said. "Mari, didn't you say that Dr. Sawyer said she had water on the brain?"

"Yes, but I'm not sure if that came from the coccidia or not," Mari said.

Leslie perked up. "Water on the brain is not a contagious illness you can just get. It usually means the dog has hydrocephalus and that's congenital. The Pet Lemon Law also says consumers have fourteen days to document contagious or infectious disease, and one year to document congenital or hereditary defects. Do you think the veterinarian documented it?"

"Even if he didn't," Emily said, feeling a jolt of energy run through her. "He will if we ask him to make it official. He was angry at the pet store, too."

Mari jumped to her feet. "I'm going to go over to the clinic right now and talk to Dr. Sawyer. Even if I don't get any money back, if we can use that report to stop Dogland from being careless in who they get their dogs from, that will be enough for me. I just don't feel at peace about Ladybug's death, and I need this. We have to make her short life count for something."

She grabbed her bag and was out the door so fast that it left Emily's head spinning.

"Wow, she's on a mission," Leslie said. "She missed the best part. At a fundraiser for the Humane Society last year, I sat next to Florida's Attorney General. We hit it off, and I have her number. When Mari gets that documentation, we'll give her a call and fill her in on what that pet store is up to."

"Good. I hope we can hit Dogland where it hurts. They need to feel some of the heat that the breeder is going to have raining down soon."

Leslie nodded in agreement, then topped off her glass and leaned back against the sofa pillows. She looked a bit distant for a moment, then turned her attention to Emily.

"I guess now we need to talk about Nico."

Chapter Nineteen

Emily nibbled on a cookie while listening to Leslie spin a tale that sounded more like something from a Disney princess movie than the experience of an American visiting Italy. While she talked, Leslie's eyes lit up and danced as though still there, Nico beside her.

"He met me at the airport with a bouquet of flowers," Leslie said. "When we arrived at his place, he had a trail of rose petals leading to my room."

"*Your* room? That sounds like he meant to be your roommate. Did he ... um—?"

Leslie laughed. "Nope, not that night. Or the next. It was another week before we had our first kiss, and it was so good that I think I saw birds swirling and chirping over my head."

Emily smiled at the vision Leslie created.

"I feel like next you're going to tell me that Nico serenaded you under your window."

"Not yet, but who knows? It could still happen," Leslie said. "But Venice, Emily, you cannot even imagine. Cars are banned on the winding, Renaissance-era streets, and we walked arm-in-arm along the cobbled lanes, Nico telling me all sorts of details about the people who had lived there back in the day. He's quite the storyteller, and I could listen to him talk for hours. He knew where all the charming back streets and hidden corners were, and he made sure we didn't miss the best ones."

Emily could only think of one word.

Uh oh.

Okay, that was two. But Leslie sounded like she was head over heels in love.

"And the gondola ride was so romantic. Our gondolier was so entertaining, with him telling us all sorts of stories about before World War II, when the head of state for Italy was a king, his lovely voice reverberating around the canal. Emily, Venice's history is fascinating! You have got to go back with me one day."

"Oh, so you're going back?" Emily asked. "When?"

Leslie was instantly somber. "I don't know. As much as I loved Italy, I missed home. Especially my dogs. And you."

Emily chuckled. "Whoa. I know I can't compare to *debonair Nico*. Let's don't go too far."

"No, I'm not saying that. But Nico had to work, and, I'll admit, the days without him were lonely."

"You didn't make any new friends, other than Nico? You were sure there long enough," Emily said, her tone scolding.

"I met Nico's friends. Communication wasn't easy, and their culture is so different than ours. Did you know that, in Italy, drip coffee is frowned upon? In the morning, the Italians have an espresso somewhere before they go to work. Nico went out and bought a coffeemaker for me, but he teased me relentlessly about it."

Emily laughed. "What does he do for a living?"

"He's a driver for a few important businessmen, and he has to be on call all sorts of hours if they need him. But he doesn't have his own car, and we drove around on a Vespa when we needed to go somewhere we couldn't walk to."

"What is a Vespa?"

"It's like a luxury Moped. You should've seen the first time he got me on it, Emily. I was terrified as he whipped in and out of traffic, driving like a madman. He laughed all the way, but I got used to it because they all drive that way."

"What was his home like?" Emily asked. So far, she couldn't determine if Nico was well off, average, or even poor.

"The homes in Italy are so different than here. It's mostly condos or apartment buildings. The older ones like where Nico lives are mostly made of stone or brick, and the newer ones are usually from concrete. They are very small, and I missed my bathtub. Tubs aren't a thing there. Also, most Italian homes don't have air conditioning and most have no yard. It's balconies everywhere for their outdoor space. I could never have my dogs there. They'd be so unhappy."

"Yes, doesn't sound very pet friendly."

Leslie grimaced. "I know I didn't paint it in a good light, but, I promise, the homes are small but so charming. And the way that the people gather for their traditional evening stroll in the center of town is just fascinating. They call it the *passeggiata*, and it's a way to touch base with your family and friends. Everyone is dressed in their finest, and sometimes we'd stop in a bar for pre-dinner snack *and coppa*. Then for dinner we'd have pasta or seafood. Or maybe breaded chicken with fennel. Of course, served with wine on the balcony as we looked over the hustle and bustle of the street below."

She looked lost in her memories.

"It sounds very much like a fairy tale," Emily said, imagining Leslie sipping her wine on the balcony.

"It was. I will never forget my time there. I think it's the way the people still include so many traditions in their everyday life. They don't forget the old ways even as they are living in a modern world. Here in America, it feels like everything old is trampled on and forgotten. People rarely hold on to traditions, and everyone is too busy to enjoy an evening walk with family and friends. We are working ourselves to death, and, in the end, what do we have?"

"So, what does all this mean, Leslie? Where do you go from here?"

Leslie put her wine glass down and sighed heavily.

"I really don't know. I invited Nico to come visit, but I doubt he'd ever leave Italy for good. And as much as I loved it over there, I can't see myself living in Italy forever. My family is here, and my business. Without doing what I do with the dogs, I don't have a purpose, and I'm not ready to let that go right now."

"Well, did you learn anything about yourself over there?" Emily asked.

"I sure did. I learned that I am worthy of love again. Whether with Nico, or someone else, or just from myself. Phillip took that confidence away from me, but my experience with Nico gave it back."

Emily smiled softly. She was so glad that Leslie had found her way out of her pity party of believing she was too old and discarded for anyone to want her again. That she had worth and would make a good life partner for someone.

"Now it's your turn to find love again," Leslie said.

Emily shook her head. She'd ruined it with Kuno, putting him in the friend zone.

Anyway, fairy tales didn't happen to people like her, and she doubted that she'd ever feel truly loved again.

"Let's switch lanes," Emily said. "We need to talk about Daisy. She's a lot, Leslie, and, to be honest with you, I just don't think I'm dog mom material."

"Oh, stop with that nonsense. You're doing great," Leslie said. "I want to hear about this cop you've been spending time with, and don't leave out any of the good parts."

Chapter Twenty

etween scrambling online trying to build a case against Dogland, working her shifts at Barks & Brews, and dealing with Daisy, it was another week before Emily got to see Valor again. But she didn't want to miss his first whole day out of the hospital, so she'd hurried over, going straight to the back yard where Kuno said they would be.

When she saw it was fenced in, she was thrilled. Perfect to keep Valor safe.

"He looks so much better," she said, rubbing him behind his ears.

Daisy was in hyper-happy mode, prancing all around Valor in Kuno's yard, trying to get his attention in the hopes he'd be a new friend for her. Leslie hadn't accepted Emily's offer of taking Daisy back and rehoming her with someone more accustomed to having dogs. She said to wait and decide when Daisy was six months old. They both knew that Leslie was buying time for Daisy to make Emily fall in love with her. If she kept making messes and trying to get off her leash during walks, that was not going to happen.

"Six days of intensive care, IV therapy, and special treatment looks good on him," Kuno said. "Dr. Sawyer's team was sad to see him go, and smothered him with hugs and kisses and new toys to keep him occupied here until they see him next week to start his heart worm treatment."

Emily had noticed a crate of dog toys and chews on the porch. Daisy had, too, grabbing one as she flew by to go meet Valor. She tossed it at him, and he walked the other way.

"What's his favorite toy?" Emily asked.

Kuno shook his head sadly. "None of them. He has no idea what to do with a toy. His obsession is food. Now that he's feeling better, he wants more and more, but we've started him on a special, monitored diet to get him back up to his proper weight slowly. Dr. Sawyer wants him to build muscle and not fat."

"That means you'd better not be feeding him from your plate," Emily teased.

"I don't," he said, a smile forming. "Much."

"Where does he sleep?"

"Wherever I tell him to," Kuno said. "He's so well behaved that it's scary. He acts like he's afraid I'll throw him out, so he has been walking around with his head down since we got home yesterday. We started him in a dog bed on the floor in my room. But he looked so lonely that I invited him up last night and, after a few hours, he accepted. I think he was scared, but he slept at my feet."

In the yard, Valor still pretended like he didn't notice Daisy, though she was right on his heels as he walked around the perimeter, marking and sniffing.

"She wants his attention," Emily said, laughing.

"That's a switcheroo, isn't it? Usually, the male is doing the chasing."

Emily gave him a playful slap on his arm. "True."

"They look fine out there," he said. "Want to go in and get something to drink? I made iced tea."

"Um ... I don't think so. I better stay near Daisy. She hasn't had her first heat yet, but she still might be able to get pregnant. I don't know enough about it to be sure."

"No worries there. Dr. Sawyer went ahead and snipped him while he had him. Valor has lost his manhood, but he still has pride."

"Aww. Poor guy has really been through it." Emily followed Kuno inside and tried to be inconspicuous about her curiosity. His house wasn't huge, but it looked neat and well-maintained. They went in through the kitchen, but, with the open concept, she could see the living room and the hallway leading to the bedrooms.

Like most guys she knew who lived alone, he'd chosen leather for his furniture. Deep brown. No throws, or pillows, but a nice rust-patterned floor rug under it all, and he did have a stack of books on his coffee table. Emily suppressed the urge to go look and see what they were about.

"This is nice," she said, then took a seat at the kitchen counter on one of his barstools.

"Thanks. I bought it ten years ago, and it was a piece of crap. I've sunk a lot of money into renovating it." He went to the fridge and pulled out a pitcher of tea, then got two glasses of ice ready. "I put in these hardwood floors myself. And those beams."

He pointed to the ceiling where there were a crisscross of dark-stained beams.

"You're a carpenter?"

"Nah—but my dad let me work with him in the summers. He was a contractor before he retired, but one that was hands on. He liked teaching the guys who worked for him, passing down his skills. He made sure I knew my way around a hammer."

"Well, you're sure adding good equity to it. Everyone wants the rustic theme these days."

"Yeah, that's what I was going for, but, to be honest, I have too many neighbors for this to be my forever home. I've always wanted a log cabin out in the country."

"I bet you could get a good price for this one, then buy your country house," she said.

He shrugged. "Maybe. But I'd also love to be near the mountains, and Florida can't give me that. But at least here, I'm near family. I see my brothers on a regular basis, and they keep me in check."

"That's important. My parents are all the way over on the west coast. Feel like they're in another world. I miss them. Are yours still living?"

He put a glass of iced tea in front of her. "Yep. My dad is still ornery as ever, too. Keeps my mom on her toes. She sends him to help me with a lot of stuff around here. Between me and my brothers, we always have something to keep him busy with."

"How many brothers do you have?" she asked, taking a sip of the tea. Any sisters?"

It was surprisingly good.

"Two. No sisters. I'm the middle child, but without the usual clichéd issues," he said, laughing. "You?"

"I've got two sisters and a brother, but coincidence here: I worked on a book about middle children several years ago."

He raised an eyebrow. "So, you know the stereotypes about my birth order are less than flattering. According to statistics, I should be an underachiever who stands sadly in the shadows of my older and younger brother, and I was overlooked as a child, leading me to be a very troubled adult. Supposedly—I mean."

Emily shook her head. "Nope. This book was called *The Secret Power of Middle Children*, and it detailed benefits of being born in the middle."

"School me," he teased, leaning forward on the counter between them.

"Hmm ... it's been a while, but I remember writing about how being the firstborn can be overwhelming because of parental expectations. Being a middle child frees you from those expectations. They can take the time to find out what they are good at themselves, without pressure. My research showed that middle children have a better sense of independence and can think out of the box easier than their siblings can."

He tilted his head, thinking. "Yeah, I guess that's true. While my older brother was trying out everything under the sun from soccer to football and failing at a lot in between before he figured out what he wanted to do, I chose baseball and stuck with it. Probably could've gotten a scholarship but I was determined to be a cop. My brother said I was nuts."

"What's he doing now?"

"Max is a sustainability program administrator. A real mouthful of a title but, basically, he leads a team that develops and puts strategies in place for the county's sustainability plan."

"I still don't know what that means," Emily said, laughing.

"Understandable. Basically, they focus on air quality, energy, waste, and all that stuff to keep the country sustainable for growth. Or something like that."

"Married?" she asked.

He nodded. "Very. They have four kids, one already in junior high. I'm the fun uncle, obviously."

He gave her a charming grin.

"Do you get along?"

"Yeah. We do, but we've had ups and downs, like brothers do. I should've known he'd be a big boss one day. Always wanted to be in charge—even when he shouldn't be. One time, when we were kids, we had a huge argument because we tried to build a homemade rocket and launch it in our backyard. Lucas, my younger brother, knew more than Max about it, but Max didn't want to give him the lead. It didn't end well, but we had a blast. No pun intended."

They both laughed.

"What's the youngest do now?" Emily asked.

"Lucas is married, too. They just had their first baby. He's an engineer in the aerospace field. Gets to play with rockets all the time now. Throws it in Max's face every chance he gets."

"Sounds like you had a good childhood."

"I did. When I wasn't refereeing between them. What about you?"

Emily remembered something else about that project. Middle children were the best negotiators. Probably did him well in his career now, too.

She was saved from diving into her own childhood by the plop of Daisy's wet nose against the sliding glass door. Valor was beside her, sheepishly waiting.

"I think we're being summoned," Kuno said, standing. "But look, they seem to get along pretty good. I'm sure he's used to being around a lot of dogs. What do you say we bring them in and let them keep each other company while we go get some lunch?"

Daisy whined at the door, her tail wagging furiously.

Emily cringed. "Are you sure about that? My girl can get kind of crazy when left alone. No telling what she might do."

Kuno looked around at his neat kitchen and living room. Then he looked back at Valor outside, standing there patiently, a short distance from Daisy. You could see the puppy energy coming off her in waves, but he was still as a statue, as though afraid it might rub off onto him.

"Okay, good point," he said. "Maybe we take her with us and give Valor a chance to rest. It's been an exciting twenty-four hours for him."

"I've got a lot to catch you up on, too," Emily said. "My friend, Leslie, is back and she's got a direct link to someone important. Someone who might just help us put Dogland out of the puppy business for good."

Chapter Twenty-One

Emily and Mari sat nervously in the opulent office at the state capital, fidgeting as they waited for their appointment with Attorney General Aria Rudy. The room exuded power and importance, with high ceilings, rich mahogany furniture, and large windows overlooking the city. It was a stark contrast to the humble origins of their cause.

Emily crossed her legs one way, then another, nervously trying to find the most comfortable but also professional angle. She plucked at the elephant on her bracelet, running her finger over the smooth metal of its trunk.

Beside her, Mari fidgeted just as much.

"I'm so sorry for the wait, but Attorney General Rudy will be with you shortly," a young man said, peeking in from the huge door before disappearing again.

"Intern," Mari said.

Emily agreed. He was too young and friendly not to be.

They'd already been waiting half an hour past their appointment time, but she wasn't complaining. She'd never dreamed that one day she would be at the state capital, advocating for dogs. She loved dogs, just like she loved every animal, but this was just not something she saw coming.

Finally, the door swung open, and Attorney General Aria Rudy entered the room. She was a striking woman with a no-nonsense demeanor. Her sharp gaze took in the two women sitting across from her, and she extended a hand in greeting.

"Good afternoon," she began, taking her seat. "I understand you have a story to share, and I'm eager to hear it. Among other passions, I'm a staunch advocate for animal rights here in Florida."

Mari began to recount their story, detailing how she had purchased a Yorkshire terrier puppy from a pet store. She handed over printed pictures of her first days with Ladybug.

"Very cute."

"Yes, she was," Mari said. "But she's gone now. Keep looking."

Attorney General Rudy flipped through the pictures, her expression growing more serious with each one.

"What pet store was this?"

When Mari revealed that they had obtained the puppy from Dogland in Dragonfly Cove, the Attorney General nodded knowingly.

"I'm not surprised. They've been skating on thin ice because I've received complaints about that pet store chain before," she admitted. "They've been warned, but I see it didn't stick."

Emily seized the opportunity to place a neatly typed paper on the desk.

"We also want to talk to you about where the store originally got Ladybug and her littermates," Emily added. "On the paper are the names and reference numbers you'll need, along with their social media profiles and website."

The Attorney General glanced at the document and then listened intently as Emily continued.

"It took getting law enforcement involved, but the manager of Dogland, Sean Broadnax, finally gave us the name of a rescue that he claimed to have purchased Mari's puppy from. I researched the rescue, and what I found out is that litter came from a woman named Lori Louise Leton, a breeder who has supplied dogs to Dogland for nearly a decade from her business called Leton Kennels in Valdosta, Georgia. After she failed multiple inspections last year, her license was revoked."

Attorney General Rudy nodded. "The GDA has recently amended several of its animal protection rules and they've been trying to squash out the worst of the breeders from doing business. But if Leton was shut down, how did she get by with providing the pet store more dogs? I'm really surprised that a national chain like Dogland would take that kind of chance to work with a breeder who has their license revoked."

"They found a loophole. Only a few months after being shut down, Leton's son applied for a 501(c)(3) status for a nonprofit rescue and was approved. Now they call it Leton's Legacy, but they're doing the exact same thing they were doing as breeders, from the same facility at the same address in Valdosta. It's the furthest thing from a rescue you could imagine. It's literally a hell hole for animals."

Attorney General Rudy leaned forward, crossing her hands together on the desk.

"Interesting. That would be called fraud."

Emily nodded. "We know that now. And reclassifying their business didn't do a thing about the way they treat their animals. I went there to check it out." She pulled her own pack of photos from her bag and put them on the desk.

Attorney General Rudy flipped through them, her face a mask of disgust.

"They're breaking almost every law. I can see that many of those cages do not even fit the minimum space required for the animals. The height of the cages must be at least six inches higher than the tallest animal in it and cannot have mesh or grated bottoms."

"Keep flipping and you'll see why those mesh floors aren't allowed any longer," Emily said.

She could tell just when Attorney General Rudy reached the photo of Valor, locked outside in the metal coop, for she paused and cursed under her breath.

"Can I keep these?" she asked. "All of them?"

Emily and Mari nodded.

Attorney General Rudy stacked both piles together and put them at the corner of her desk. She looked like she was simmering with anger.

"Now," she said. "Let's get the ball rolling here. The fact that they're in Georgia is complicated, but not insurmountable. Have you contacted the Department of Agriculture Protection Division?"

"I did, and they said it needed to be handled at a local level, so a friend of mine has a contact in the Valdosta Sheriff's Office. Law enforcement is coordinating with the local Humane Society to plan a task force operation to catch Lori Louise Leton and her son off guard."

"Depending on how many dogs are there, they'll need a backup rescue to take some," the Attorney General said. "There are a lot of details to pull together for something like this."

"Right. It's a whole big thing. They're calling it *Operation Valor*. My friend said they have a rescue lined up to work with the Humane Society to seize the dogs and place them somewhere safe. Unfortunately, it was supposed to happen this week, but was pushed back yet another week due to scheduling conflicts."

Attorney General Rudy sighed, her expression sympathetic. "Like I often say, the wheels of justice turn slow, unfortunately," she said. "But there's more we can do. On this end, we'll tackle the pet store situation. I've got to make some calls, gather some facts, and it'll be a few weeks or more, but, trust me, my team will be on it."

She went on to explain that the Consumer Protection Division of her office had the authority to pursue individuals and entities engaged in unfair trade practices or deceptive methods.

The intern popped in again and tapped his watch, and AG Rudy stood.

"Thank you so much for bringing this to my attention, ladies. Stephen will show you out," she said. "You two should get ready because, by the time I'm done with the Dogland Pet Store chain, heads are going to roll."

Leaving the Attorney General's office, Emily and Mari remained composed as they walked down the halls of the state capital. However, as soon as they stepped outside and reached the sidewalk, their emotions overcame them.

Emily turned to Mari and held her arms out wide.

"Yes!" she shouted, feeling a rush of exhilaration.

Mari hugged her and shouted with pure elation, drawing strange looks from passersby.

When they finally calmed down and pulled away from their jubilant embrace, they headed to the parking lot.

"Emily, I can't thank you enough for everything," Mari said. "It feels amazing to be a part of something like this. Something I can really be proud of."

Emily had to agree with her. Using her strengths for

more than just writing a book about the benefits of vegetables was feeling good. The passion she'd felt the night before, writing her report about the Leton's Legacy situation was something she'd been hoping to find again in her work. Her fingers had flown across the keyboard, dancing effortlessly with the emotions that went into all she'd seen and needed to convey to someone else with her words.

She'd felt like a true writer. Even if just for a moment.

Chapter Twenty-Two

Emily stood and stretched, reaching her fingers toward the ceiling of her kitchen. She really needed to get a desk and chair set up. In the past, she'd always worked all over the house, dragging her laptop from the couch to the kitchen table, and even to coffee shops. She still liked to do that and had found a nice spot to work from at the dog park across the street when Daisy needed exercising, but, now that she'd found her muse and was furiously trying to get everything out of her head and onto the page, she was working for longer intervals and her body was screaming out for a proper set up.

In the last few months, her life was busier than usual. It was also June in Florida and too hot to work outside unless it was early morning, and Emily didn't do early mornings.

Between working her shifts at Barks & Brews, helping with Valor when Kuno was on shift, and pounding out chapters for her secret writing project, it felt like she was on a series of roller coasters, barely time to disembark and get in line for the next one.

She could barely make time for Leslie, who was struggling now that she'd come home, glad to be there but missing Nico and wondering if she'd made a huge mistake. Half the time she needed to vent in person, Emily wasn't there because she was spending a lot of time at Kuno's house. Thankfully, he had good Wi-Fi, and she could work from there just as comfortably as she could from her own home, so they could make sure that Valor wasn't left alone for too long. His recovery was going well, but at times he got weak and needy.

Other times, he was finding his youth again.

She smiled, thinking of him and Daisy trotting around the perimeter of the backyard together. "You love you some Valor, don't you," she teased Daisy, rubbing at her belly with her foot. "You think he's your boyfriend, huh?"

Daisy's ears perked at hearing Valor's name.

Turns out that ole Valor finally gave in, and accepted Daisy's crazy spirit, and, when she came over, he followed her around, emulating some of her antics in his attempt to act like a dog. For so many years he just existed in a cage, so he hadn't known about hiking his leg to mark bushes, or chew on a toy, or just wallow and roll on his back in the grass, enjoying the sunshine.

But Daisy was easily showing him the ropes. Kuno said Valor acted mopey until Daisy came back around, and that he instantly perked up when he heard Emily's car come up. Most of the time, Kuno wasn't there when Emily was supervising the two dogs, but he popped in and out with lunch when he could.

Emily's phone dinged and she went to pick it up.

There was a text from Kuno.

Operation Valor. Tonight @ 10. I'll keep you updated.

Emily lowered herself slowly onto the couch. She could feel her pulse fluttering in her heart, suddenly excited that at least part of the shutdown was going to finally happen.

Attorney General Aria Rudy was hitting some road-blocks on her end, as well as gathering more reports of ill or dying dogs purchased from Dogland. She wanted to have as many plaintiffs as she could before pouncing, she said. To make matters more anxiety-building, every time Kuno turned around, Jimmy was giving him news that they had to reschedule the sting. With so many moving parts, it was complicated, Kuno said.

He was much calmer about it than Emily, who couldn't stop thinking about all those dogs there, being neglected and forgotten, until they needed to be bred or sold.

Mari was also frustrated, and was going to be thrilled at the update.

Emily texted her.

Tonight. Operation Valor Confirmed.

Mari replied immediately.

Let's go stealth. They don't have to see us.

Emily started to send a text back to refuse, and even began typing, but she paused.

Seeing Ronald and his mother taken away in handcuffs would be the ultimate payoff from all the stress of the last few months. It could be a memory she could hold onto forever, especially every time she saw Valor stumble or look confused at how to be a real dog.

Yes, she'd grown very attached to the German Shepherd. She'd even offered to take him, but Kuno was also fond of him and didn't want to let him go.

There was a look in his eyes now when he looked at them. A look of gratitude that she'd never seen a dog display. An expression of love and loyalty that told her he'd give his life for either of them. She and Kuno were now walking the two dogs to the park occasionally, and Valor was always on alert, as though he'd figured out that his breed was a protector, while Daisy was meant to be an entertainer.

Emily loved him.

Valor—not Kuno.

She and Kuno were just friends. Emily was a bit irritated, though, because, despite her pleading her case once again, Kuno confirmed that she couldn't be there during Operation Valor. That she couldn't be a part of taking down *Leton's Legacy*. She didn't see why she couldn't come if there were also going to be people there from the Humane Society and another rescue. She felt like he was just being overprotective.

Another text came through.

> I hear you thinking about it over there.

> Just say yes.

Valdosta, Georgia, after dark, was scarier than Emily had anticipated, and the woods around the Leton property were downright terrifying.

Right on cue, they heard a coyote howl in the distance, then a chorus of barking and yelps, his posse on the trail to find their leader.

"That sounds far away," she said to Mari, lying through her teeth.

"Hopefully."

Mari had talked her into coming, or at least that was going to be Emily's defense in case Kuno found out. But he should never be the wiser because he thought she was at his home with Valor and Daisy.

Emily owed Leslie big time and the only reason she'd relented in standing in for Emily was because she was such a romantic that she thought it was sweet that Emily was worried for Kuno and wanted to be there, watching from a discreet place.

Or at least that was the story that Emily fed her to get her to dog-sit.

Leslie had texted her no less than six or seven times

during the three-hour ride to Georgia, saying she was bored there. Emily told her to just hang loose until it was late enough to call Nico in Italy, who would keep her busy on the phone for at least a few hours.

They'd nearly been late after being held up by a fender bender on the highway just a few miles from where they turned off to get to the Leton property. But, so far, no one was there.

"Are you sure this is happening tonight?" Mari asked.

"Positive."

Emily couldn't see Mari's face. It was that dark and they only used their phone flashlights to get into the woods without breaking their necks and finding a huge fallen oak to take cover behind. Mari was afraid that shooting might break out, while Emily was more concerned with being seen, and it was going to be hard to see from the distance they'd chosen, but it was safer than being caught lurking in the trees.

"I feel like a ninja," Mari said, giggling.

They'd both dressed in black for their covert adventure. Leggings, shirts, and shoes. Emily had to admit, this was the most exciting thing she'd been a part of in longer than she could remember.

"You look like one, too," Emily said. "Just don't get any ideas. We are to remain invisible. Kuno would be so furious if he knew we were here."

At precisely 9.45 p.m., a beat-up truck and a sleek, red sports car pulled up to the facility. Emily observed Ronald Gettlefinger and a woman, presumably his mother, emerging from the vehicles and unlocking the facility's door, then going in.

Emily couldn't help but mutter her disdain for Ronald under her breath.

"That's Ronald," she whispered. "Scumbag extraordinaire."

Mari leaned closer and inquired, "How did they manage to get here at this hour?"

Emily replied in hushed tones, "Kuno said that an undercover officer set up a meeting with them at a nearby park for 10:30 p.m., pretending to be interested in buying two purebred Labradoodles. They'd have to come here to get the dogs to make the exchange."

Mari then asked, "But why conduct this operation at night?"

Emily guessed, "I think it's easier for them to move around under the cover of darkness, less likely to be seen. His mother probably agreed because she's able to sell two at one time. Their greed will get them to do anything at any time of the day."

As they continued to wait in silence, the distant sound of a convoy of cars speeding up the road caught their attention. Six county patrol vehicles, accompanied by civilian cars and white vans, pulled up to the facility. Law enforcement officers emerged and signaled for the civilians to remain in place. Emily's keen eye caught the outline of a man she recognized as Kuno, looking rather dashing in his tight, black attire.

A team of a dozen uniformed officers entered the facility, while others stood guard outside. Shouts echoed from within, and Emily couldn't help but worry for Kuno's safety. However, her fears were alleviated as she watched Kuno exit the building, pushing Ronald forward in handcuffs.

Jimmy followed closely, escorting a struggling and cursing Lori Leton. The officers swiftly placed them in separate patrol cars.

Unable to contain their excitement any longer, Emily

and Mari exchanged a silent but triumphant high-five. An officer signaled to the group of waiting civilians, and people began to emerge from their vehicles. They carried crates, stacking them outside the facility's door, ready for action.

Emily overheard a woman's voice describing the facility as one of the worst puppy mills she had ever seen. Her friend agreed, and they carried small, white Pomeranians in their arms.

One of the dogs squirmed vigorously.

"She's going to drop that dog," Emily predicted.

Sure enough, the dog slipped from the woman's grasp and made a mad dash for the woods, straight toward Mari and Emily.

The woman pushed the other dog into a crate, kicking it shut before taking off, giving chase to the dog.

"Crap, they're coming this way," Mari hissed at Emily.

"Don't move. Just be quiet."

As Emily watched the chase, it was evident that the woman had no chance to catch the fast, little pup. It was already almost to them, while she was fumbling through branches and trees.

What if the dog wasn't caught? It would be coyote feed!

In a swift move, Emily lunged forward and managed to catch the dog just before it reached the woods, but she had to reveal herself to do it.

The woman who had been chasing the dog stopped.

"Who the hell are you and why are you hiding out here like a criminal?" she asked, breathless and sweaty.

Chapter Twenty-Three

A full month after *Operation Valor* was successfully conducted, and Lori Louise Leton and her son, Ronald, were jailed with a hundred-thousand-dollar bond each on charges of felony animal cruelty, Emily stood with Mari and Leslie on the street in front of the Dogland store, ready to watch the press conference.

"Here she comes," Mari said, elbowing Emily.

They watched as Attorney General Aria Rudy was helped from a black Suburban, then followed to where a team had set up microphones, cameras encircling them like vultures.

Rudy was dressed in a slim-fitting dark suit, white blouse, and 3-inch red heels. Her expression was stoic, and she looked like she was out for blood.

Emily could see the manager, Sean Broadnax, huddled at the doors of the store with a few employees. He scowled with anger, but there was nothing he could do about what was happening.

The only thing that would make the situation more satisfying was if Kuno were there with them. But finding out that she'd gone against him and was at Operation Valor had not only angered him but also disappointed him and broken their trust.

They hadn't spoken since that night. Kuno didn't respond to her text messages or her calls, so she finally stopped trying.

Emily missed Valor dearly. It was evident that Daisy did, too.

She fiddled with her bracelet, tracing the tiny elephant with her finger. If only Mari hadn't talked her into going to Valdosta that night. After they'd been discovered in the woods, Kuno had approached and, when he saw it was Emily and Mari, he'd grabbed both of their arms and practically dragged them out of the tree line and placed them in the backseat of his car. He'd climbed into the front and lectured them on all the ways things could've gotten bad and they could've been hurt, and how it would've been his fault because he'd disclosed the event to Emily.

She had never seen him so angry, but she had to give it to him. He'd remained calm and collected as he—without any qualms—told them to get back to Florida, then drove them to their car located a mile away. He hadn't given Emily any sort of indication he'd call her later.

Four weeks—and not a word.

Attorney General Aria Rudy stepped up to the microphone and held her hand up, asking for silence before she began. "Today we've filed a formal complaint against Dogland, Inc. and its owners for misrepresentation to consumers that the animals they sell are healthy, high-quality animals, and fit for sale, when, in fact, in some instances, puppies have died soon after being purchased or suffered from congenital or other hereditary disorders. We now have sixteen plaintiffs who purchased puppies from

Dogland either via their online store or in person at this location, and soon discovered the dogs were very sick. These dogs presented with numerous illnesses including canine parvovirus, Giardia, coccidia, bacterial pneumonia, and intussusception, as well as numerous congenital disorders including eye defects, blindness, hip dysplasia, luxating patella, inefficient lungs, and, in Ms. Sanchez's puppy's case, hydrocephalus."

Murmurs went through the crowd, and she quieted them again.

"One complainant reported that when she saw a puppy vomiting in a pen at the store and asked what was wrong with it, she was told that the puppy was nervous or excited to see the consumer and that vomiting was normal behavior for puppies."

She paused, shaking her head in disgust.

"Furthermore, the sale of sick and dying puppies is both immoral and illegal. Planning for a new puppy requires a great deal of time and money—and certainly there is an emotional investment. Families deserve the assurance that they will in fact receive the high-quality puppy they were promised. It is disgraceful that the defendants would exploit the trust of new pet owners to make a profit while risking the health and safety of these puppies. Recently a puppy was sold to a resident of Dragonfly Cove from this store, and it died a week later. An investigation proved that the puppy and its littermates were purchased by Dogland from a puppy mill in Georgia." She nodded at an assistant nearby and an enlarged poster of Ladybug at her sickest was unveiled. Then she looked out into the crowd until she spotted Emily and Mari and asked them to come forward.

Emily's knees were knocking when they got up there, and Rudy introduced them.

"This is Mari Sanchez, the consumer who bought Ladybug. And this is her friend, Emily Doxon, who made it possible to uncover what the Letons were doing, and the atrocious conditions of their facility—which has been evacuated. All the dogs are now safe, and the puppy mill owners are facing numerous charges, including cruelty to animals."

"How were they able to do this under Florida's strict animal protection laws?" a reporter asked.

"Because the defendants had their USDA breeder's license revoked and immediately applied to turn their business into a 501(c)(3) rescue. In addition to putting the dogs on their website and charging exorbitant so-called adoption fees for them, they continued to provide Dogland with hundreds of dogs, though under their new foundation classification. While they sold the puppies for a few hundred dollars or so to Dogland, the store turned around and sold them from anywhere between fifteen hundred dollars to, in a couple cases, more than eight thousand. It amounts to nothing short of puppy laundering."

Almost in unison, the crowd turned to the pet store, in a glare of condemnation before they returned their attention to Rudy. Emily saw Sean Broadnax turn and flounce back into his store.

"Next, I'll be hand-delivering an injunction to the manager of Dogland, preventing them from participating in further deception while this case is being sorted out through legal channels," she said.

Rudy continued. "We'll leave this here as a message to all pet stores and backyard breeders. We plan to protect our citizens from violations under the Florida Deceptive and Unfair Trade Practices Act, and we will be seeking restitution and reimbursements to consumers. If anyone else around the state has done business with Dogland, Inc., and ended up with an ill dog, or lost one to death, please contact my office."

With that she quietly said goodbye to Emily and Mari, then turned on her heels and left the microphone as photographers snapped furiously.

"Well, that was exciting," Mari said, grinning from ear to ear.

Emily couldn't respond. The crowd had started disbursing and, with its thinning, she saw Kuno with his arms crossed, leaning back against his patrol car about a quarter of a mile away.

Other vehicles were pulling away, but he made no motion to move. He was looking straight toward her, his gaze unwavering.

But he was too far away for her to read his expression.

"Mari, I'll meet you at the car," Emily said. "I see someone I need to talk to."

As though he'd heard what she said and knew her intention, he turned slowly and got into his car, then drove toward where she and Mari stood at the curb.

Emily was frozen in place as he drove past her, his eyes focused on the road ahead of him. He didn't even tap the brakes. No wave.

Nothing.

She felt Mari's arms around her shoulders in a reassuring hug.

"Men are stupid," Mari murmured. "Come on. Let's go have a glass of wine."

Chapter Twenty-Four

Wet Your Whistle Wednesdays at Barks & Brews were usually a nightmare for Emily because she was normally waiting tables. Offering two cocktails for the price of one brought out all the girls around town who used the discounted evening as their weekly Ladies Night outing.

This time, Emily was one of them, having agreed to work Saturday night for Katie who was now working her Wednesday.

It wasn't only ladies there, though. There were plenty of single men who were smart enough to pick the right night to come out. One of them had asked Emily if he could buy her a drink, but she'd declined. He'd had blue eyes like Kuno, but Emily's heart just wasn't in it for playing the game.

She hadn't seen or talked to Kuno in three months now. It was as if they'd never met, other than the massive amount of time that Emily spent regretting her actions that had made him and Valor disappear from her life. On some days, she genuinely felt like she was going crazy. Usually, with a problem she was dealing with, she'd go to Leslie for advice.

And she still might, but, right now, she was still ashamed at how she'd singlehandedly ruined the good friendship she had with Kuno.

Leslie and Mari had hit it off, and chattered on and on without her. Mari was telling Leslie all about Mushu, her pet Bearded Dragon. She'd decided that until she'd graduated college, it wasn't responsible to get another dog. She was having a good time training her dragon to walk on a leash and loved all the attention she got with him on campus.

Marigold and Mushu. Sounded like a sitcom.

Emily watched the enclosed dog area while they chatted, keeping an eye on Daisy. She was ecstatic to be there, playing with other dogs, unlike Emily, who didn't even want to be out and about, no matter where it was. It would've been amazing to stay home in her baggy pajamas, eating ice cream and binging on Netflix with Daisy, or putting the final polish on her writing project that she'd just finished the day before. However, her two most irritating friends refused to allow that, so here they were, on their second round of mojitos, which meant now Emily was going to have to get an Uber home.

"Then he sent me a screen shot," Leslie said, throwing her hands in the air as though she was helpless to do anything about it.

"Wait—" Emily said. "I missed that. Screenshot of what?"

"His flight itinerary, to come visit me. Jeez ... where are you tonight, Em? Have you heard anything I've said? Nico said he can't live without me and he's coming to Florida in three weeks."

"That's great," Emily said, smiling. She was glad that Nico was coming. Leslie wouldn't admit it, but she was smitten with him and had been heartsick since leaving him behind in Italy.

"He's probably going to drag you back to his country, kicking and screaming," Mari said. "Aren't Italians overly macho?"

Emily had to laugh at the vision Mari created. Sounded more caveman than Italian.

"I think you've been watching too many mafia movies, Mari. Nico isn't macho," Leslie said. "He's all sugar."

"Doesn't he need to apply for a visa before he can come?" Emily asked.

"No," Leslie said. "Italy is part of the Visa Waiver Program, and Italian citizens can travel to the United States without a visa for a stay up to ninety days."

"Wow," Emily said. "He's staying three months?"

"I don't know about that. For now, we're just planning a few weeks. I have a feeling his culture shock is going to be so deep that he'll be running back to Italy with his tail between his legs," Leslie said. "On that note, I need to find a good espresso machine."

"Speaking of tail between the legs," Mari said. "Looks like that dog isn't a regular here. He's scared and doesn't like all the attention. Oh, wait, there goes Daisy to the rescue."

Emily and Leslie looked over to where Mari pointed.

When she saw the dog in question, she nearly flew off the barstool and jogged over to the enclosure, slipping through the gate.

"Valor!" she exclaimed, kneeling, and enveloping the dog in her arms. "Where have you been, boy?"

He was just as happy to see her, his tail wagging furiously as he tongue-whipped her face. Daisy tried to push through under Emily's arms, jealous that she was getting all Valor's attention.

"We've been around."

Emily looked up from where she now sat on the ground, legs splayed, as Valor and Daisy rolled around against her.

Kuno towered over her.

"I Ii," she said, coming to her feet and taking the opportunity to hide the shock on her face while she brushed the dog hair from her black jeans.

"Hi," he returned.

She had to face him, and, when she stood to her full height, only inches from him, she felt small and at a loss for words. Kuno hated her. And that didn't feel good. Not at all.

"How have you been?" she finally said.

"Busy. I decided to put my house on the market after all. Turns out there was a lot to be done to it before I could list it. I've been buried under small projects."

"Oh. So, you've found your log cabin, huh?"

He shook his head. "No, not yet. But I'm looking. I think Valor would do better out of the city and surrounded by nature. I think I would, too."

She smiled. "I'm sure you both would. There's nothing like country life, I've heard. I hope you find those mountains you're looking for, Kuno."

They stood there awkwardly for a moment.

"Can you take a break and chat with me for a few minutes?" he asked. "I have something I want to tell you."

"I'm not working tonight. Leslie and Mari made me come. They said I've been spending too much time home alone. Well, with Daisy, I mean. But, yes—I can chat."

They went to a tall table and stood opposite each other. When Katie came by, Kuno ordered a beer and Emily asked for a coffee. When she disappeared, they didn't say anything at first.

"Leton's Legacy is shut down for good," he said finally. "Not sure if you heard about it, but the building is going to be demolished. They sold the property to pay their legal fees."

"I hadn't heard, but that's wonderful. I hope all the dogs got good homes."

He nodded. "It wasn't easy, but, yes, most of them have been permanently placed. We ended up seizing over six hundred dogs that night. It took us several weeks to get all of them ready to be adopted. Many were horribly matted. Some had ear and eye infections, badly irritated skin, upper respiratory infections, and a whole slew of other medical concerns. Despite all of that, they were all in good spirits the morning after the sting operation. I think they knew they were going to be taken care of. Jimmy said that they lost twelve of them in the next days, though. Some of them just couldn't hold on anymore."

Emily wiped away tears, thinking of the abuse some of the dogs had suffered.

"I don't think you got enough credit for what you did for those dogs, Emily," he said softly. "If not for you, no one would've been the wiser of what was going on there. How does it feel to collar your first criminals?"

"I didn't collar them. You did. And I don't need credit," Emily said. "My reward is knowing they aren't there suffering any longer. And it was a team effort, Kuno. If you hadn't have gone with me, I might not have made any sort of headway, and they'd still be there."

He smiled sadly.

"I know I've acted like a brat," he said.

She looked away. He had acted like a brat, and it hurt.

"When I saw you coming out of those woods, it scared me so badly. Both Ronald and Lori Leton were packing,

Emily. We caught them by surprise, and they didn't draw their weapons, but they could've. And the what-could've-happened scenarios played in my mind, and I was angry at myself. Angry for dragging you into something that wasn't safe. I really wasn't angry at you."

Emily shook her head. "Not true. I know when anger is pointed at me. And at the press conference, even though you didn't look at me when you drove by, I could see the daggers. You were stone cold and that cut me deep, Kuno."

"Because by then, I'd let it go on so long that I didn't know what to say. I've never felt this way and I've cussed myself every day and night since Operation Valor. But I couldn't go another day without coming here to apologize. I'm sorry, Emily."

She met his gaze, even as she was wiping the tears from her eyes.

"Apology accepted. And again, I'm sorry for going to Valdosta when you told me to stay away. I broke our trust, and it's weighed on me heavily."

"Accepted."

"So how has the vegetable book been going?" Kuno asked.

She raised her eyebrows, laughing. "It's not. I told her I couldn't finish it. Instead, I woke up one day with an idea, and it was like my fingers were on fire. I've never worked on something I believe in so much. And it's almost done. I have an agent who is waiting for it. She read a partial and thinks she can sell it. But—who knows—probably not."

"Don't say that. You'll send bad vibes into the universe. Think positive and it'll happen. Want to share what it's about?"

"Well," she said, smiling. It's called *Saving Valor: A Shepherd's Story*, and it's all about you know who."

Right on cue, Valor arrived at their feet and lay down in front of Kuno, with Daisy bringing up the rear. They looked pleased with themselves.

"Wow. A book about my dog," Kuno said. "That's so cool. I'm so proud of you for going off track and doing something you feel passionate about. That's exactly what you needed."

"Thanks," Emily said, feeling bashful about the project now. "How is he doing?"

"Valor? Oh, he's great. We have one more heart worm treatment, and his hips and that front paw will always give him trouble from being in that wire coop for so many years, but he's as good as can be expected. And he's happy."

"Good. He deserves it. I've missed him." She hopped off her stool and kneeled again, hugging Valor, rubbing his sore hip.

Kuno also came and knelt next to them.

"Did you miss me, too?" he asked.

They were both on their knees, their faces only inches apart.

Emily wasn't sure how to answer that. If she admitted how much she missed him, she would only sound pathetic. But if she didn't, that was just one more way of breaking trust. Relationships built with lies only crumbled. She knew that firsthand.

"Yes. I've missed you," she whispered.

He looked down at the elephant bracelet on her wrist, looking somber. "Can I have that back?"

Her heart sank. "My bracelet? Why?"

"Because we said it's a friendship bracelet, and I don't think we are friends anymore."

Katie came by, saw how serious they were, and kept going. Dogs ran around them, and Daisy tried to snuggle with Valor. The band struck up a rendition of "All of Me," by John Legend, the house lead singer crooning the words.

Everything kept moving around them, but all Emily could think of was that Kuno didn't want to be her friend. This wasn't just a bump in the road.

It was really over.

She attempted to undo the clasp of the bracelet. Before she could get it undone, there was suddenly a sparkle in front of her face.

"I guess you can keep the bracelet, though I was going to trade it for this," Kuno said. "I don't want you to be my friend. I want you to be my wife. I don't know where I'll find my log cabin, or a mountain to gaze at, but I don't want to do it alone."

She was speechless.

He continued. "When we were in Valdosta, you told me something your grandmother used to say. '*Love is not running away or giving up, it's staying and fighting for every single moment you have together.*' I messed up and stopped fighting for us, and I wasted a lot of moments, but I'm back. And this time I'm not giving up. Emily Doxon, I can't live without you and Valor can't live without Daisy. Will the two of you marry the two of us?"

The ring had somehow got the attention of the table next to them, and, with a few comments here and there, they had a circle of people standing around them, including Leslie and Mari, who were grinning so hard their faces looked frozen. Beside Leslie stood Nora Anderson, holding the leash to her dog, Charlie.

Emily didn't look at any of them. She didn't need any advice. This time she knew exactly what to do. She wasn't crazy. Well, not insane, but she *was* crazy in love with Kuno, and had been since the moment she'd met him.

She wished her grandmother could see her now.

"Yes," she said, pulling Kuno's face in and kissing him on the lips. "We'll marry you."

The End

Thank you for reading *Collar Me Crazy*, the second book in the Dragonfly Cove Dog Park series. In the next books, you'll get to see more of Emily, Kuno, and more characters you've met here. In addition, if you'd like to see where Kuno finds his dream house and his mountain, you can find him featured in my *Hart's Ridge* series [here]. But first, I think you'll want to check out the next book in the *Dragonfly Cove Dog Park* series. I guarantee you'll want to meet Marsha and her dog, Earl, in *Hearts Unleashed*, by Tammy L. Grace.

BOOK 3: HEARTS UNLEASHED by Tammy L. Grace

Welcome to the dog-friendly town of Dragonfly Cove, where you'll find plenty of heartwarming moments that blend canine companionship into the everyday lives of ordinary people, to create extraordinary stories. If you loved books like *Wish Me Home* by Kay Bratt, the *Second Chance* series by Casey Wilson, and the *Guiding Emily* series by Barbara Hinske, you will enjoy the books in the bestselling Dragonfly Cove Dog Park series, all heartwarming stories of the dogs who rescue us!

Hearts Unleashed, by USA Today bestselling author Tammy L. Grace, is the next book in the Dragonfly Cove Dog Park series. Embark on a heart-wrenching journey with Marsha Warner as she grapples with grief and a secret buried for far too long. In the wake of her most recent loss,

Marsha finds solace and a glimmer of hope in the form of Earl, an adorable puppy, who holds the key to healing her shattered heart. As Marsha trains Earl and expands her social circle, the secret that has weighed on her for years bubbles to the surface. With the encouragement of her newfound friends and the unwavering loyalty of Earl, Marsha summons the courage to take a chance—one that promises profound happiness or unimaginable heartbreak. *Hearts Unleashed* is a feel-good tale of love, resilience, and the transformative power of second chances.

The Dragonfly Cove Dog Park series is perfect for fans of women's fiction who love stories that are as heartwarming as they are entertaining.

★ Don't miss any of the Dragonfly Cove books! Download them all today! ★

Book 1: Pick of the Litter

Book 2: Collar Me Crazy by Kay Bratt

Book 3: Hearts Unleashed by Tammy L. Grace

Book 4: Back in the Pack by Barbara Hinske

Book 5: Loyal & True by Ev Bishop

Book 6: Coming Home to Heel by Jodi Allen Brice

Book 7: Unleashed Melody by Julie Carobini

Book 8: Teacher's Pet by David Johnson

Book 9: A New Leash on Life by Patricia Sands

Note from the Author

Hello, readers! Wow, I've had so much fun writing *Collar Me Crazy*, the 2nd book in the *Dragonfly Cove Dog Park* series! This is my third time working on a multi-author series, and the collaboration is the best part. In the following books of Dragonfly Cove Dog Park, you'll get to see many cameos from crossover characters, businesses you've become familiar with, and all the fun tidbits we created to build the fictional town of Dragonfly Cove.

The best part about it is that right now you can get all the books in the series, without waiting! And if you've enjoyed *Collar Me Crazy*, I would appreciate so much if you'd show your love in an Amazon review, and Goodreads and BookBub, if you are feeling really generous. The more reviews these books get, the more excited we will be to consider expanding the series.

You can also learn more about how Kuno and Emily's life pans out in my own series, Hart's Ridge. Their story is a few books in, so be patient as you move through them! And I invite you to join my private Facebook group, Kay's Krew, where you can be part of my focus group, giving ideas for story details such as names, livelihoods, etc. to this series. I'm also known to entertain with stories of my life with the Bratt Pack and all the kerfuffles I find myself getting into. Please join my author newsletter to hear of future *Hart's Ridge* books, as well as giveaways and discounts.

Until then,

Scatter kindness everywhere.

Kay Bratt

About the Author

Writer, Rescuer, Wanderer

Kay Bratt is the powerhouse author behind over 30 internationally bestselling books that span genres from mystery and women's fiction to memoir and historical fiction. Her books are renowned for delivering an emotional wallop wrapped in gripping storylines. Her Hart's Ridge small-town mystery series earned her the coveted title of Amazon All Star Author and continues to be one of her most successful projects out of her more than million books sold around the world.

Kay's literary works have sparked lively book club discussions wide-reaching, with her works translated into multiple languages, including German, Korean, Chinese, Hungarian, Czech, and Estonian.

Beyond her writing, Kay passionately dedicates herself to rescue missions, championing animal welfare as the former Director of Advocacy for Yorkie Rescue of the Carolinas. She considers herself a lifelong advocate for children, having volunteered extensively in a Chinese orphanage and supported nonprofit organizations like An Orphan's Wish (AOW), Pearl River Outreach, and Love Without Boundaries. In the USA, Kay served as a Court

Appointed Special Advocate (CASA) for abused and neglected children in Georgia, as well as spearheaded numerous outreach programs for underprivileged kids in South Carolina.

As a wanderlust-driven soul, Kay has called nearly three dozen different homes on two continents her own. Her globetrotting adventures have taken her to captivating destinations across Mexico, Thailand, Malaysia, China, the Philippines, Central America, the Bahamas, and Australia. Today, she and her soulmate of 30 years find their sanctuary by the serene banks of Lake Hartwell in Georgia, USA.

Described as southern, spicy, and a touch sassy, Kay loves to share her life's antics with the Bratt Pack on social media. Follow her on Facebook, Twitter, and Instagram to join the fun.

For more information, visit www.kaybratt.com.